# TURNCOAT . . .

Steele was drifting west again, after being as far in the east as he had ever been since he set out on the vengeance trail in pursuit of his father's killers.

New Orleans had been the place where his eastward drift had ended. And there had been women trouble of the worst kind in the city and the delta country of the Mississippi's lower reaches. He had gone there with the intention of raising money. He had a small stake, which he hoped to build on at the poker tables of the plush hotels. But there had been another woman, which was nothing new. And deceit and violence and death—as he had known, deep down, that there would be.

The Virginian hated no one unless he had a personal reason, so he felt no repugnance against professional killers as a breed. But he had always fought shy of becoming one himself.

Now, for the first time since he had placed himself outside the law, Steele was about to become a gun for hire. . . .

## THE ADAM STEELE SERIES:

No. 16
George G. Gilman

ADAM STEELE

NIGHTMARE AT NOON

PINNACLE BOOKS          LOS ANGELES

ADAM STEELE #16: NIGHTMARE AT NOON

*Copyright © 1978 by George G. Gilman*

Pinnacle Books edition, published by special arrangement with New English Library, Ltd.

First printing, July 1980

ISBN: 0-523-40526-X

Cover illustration by Fred Love

*Printed in the United States of America*

PINNACLE BOOKS, INC.
2029 Century Park East
Los Angeles, California 90067

For Peter Ellis: Welcome to the club

# NIGHTMARE AT NOON

# CHAPTER ONE

The girl sat on a three-legged stool in the doorway of the padre's house and fanned her face and breasts with part of a mail order catalog. Stirring the oven-heated air did little to cool her filthy and sweat-tacky flesh; but it helped to keep the angrily buzzing flies off her.

Her name was Caroline Keyes and she was in her early twenties. Even she did not know her precise age. But she was aware that she possessed a beautiful face and a fine figure. Although she was making anything but the best of her femininity now as she sighed, rose from the stool and stepped down off the stoop of the padre's house.

Her shoulders were hunched and she dragged her naked feet over the flagstone walk across the barren garden and then through the thick layer of dust on the street: her careless gait in keeping with her slovenly appearance.

She was slimly built and two inches above five feet tall. Her flame-red satin gown trimmed with white lace had been expensive, but was never designed for long and hard wear. It fitted snugly to her slender waist, the way it was supposed to. But it should have reached down to her ankles, curving out over many petticoats. Just as it should have been fastened with pearl buttons to the top of the bodice—to reveal just the beginning of

1

her cleavage. When it had been new, the sleeves of the dress had been long.

Such a gown would have been ideal for a beautiful woman to wear at a big city ball. But Rain, Texas was not a big city. And, even in its heyday, there had never been so much as a barn dance in the meeting hall across from the padre's house.

Since Caroline reached town, there had been no single second in any day or night for which the gown was suitable. But it was the only dress she possessed and, after a week of heat and dust and sweat and squalor, she had adapted it to her needs. The petticoats—and everything else she had worn beneath the gown—had been dispensed with. Then the lower part of the full skirt had ben ripped off so that the ragged edge hung only to mid-calf level. The sleeves were torn away from the shoulder stitchings to leave her arms bare. During the heat of the day—and it was constantly blisteringly hot in Rain from sun-up to dusk—she left the bodice unfastened to the waist to expose both her firm, conical, dark-crested breasts in the tapering, lace-trimmed vee.

As she ambled slowly towards the eastern end of Rain's single street, she continued to move the pages of the catalog back and forth in front of her face. A face made up of well-formed features, each complementing the others to present a delicately unified whole. The bone structure was discreet and even the sweat-moist dirt ingrained in the pores and the shallow lines around her mouth and at the corners of her eyes did not detract from her beauty. Neither did the dullness of her pale green eyes. Nor even the tangled and greasy condition of the blonde hair which fell thickly down her back to reach the base of her spine.

These signs of neglect merely added up to a different kind of beauty: perhaps an even more exciting kind.

2

For, if a woman could look so good without making the slightest effort, what would she be like if she tried?

But Caroline's attraction was only apparent at a distance as she reached the eastern end of the street and turned wearily around to start back the way she had come. And it would simply have been in the eye of the beholder had anyone been able to see her. Up close, she stank. Which was why the big flies continued to trail her, risking the swatting catalog fan for a chance to taste the rancid sweat of her exposed flesh.

Nobody could see her beauty or smell her taint, though, for she had been totally alone in Rain ever since she rode into town on the west trail, except for the big blue flies, the jack rabbits, and the coyotes. And, with a human presence, the animals had deserted town, leaving just the girl and the flies.

"About time, you sonofabitch friggin' bastard!" the girl snarled.

Her harsh tone was a match for the profane words. The opening and closing of her sensuously pouted mouth robbed her entire face of its beauty. Not because of the contribution it made to the sneer of bitter hatred, but instead, because the parting of her lips revealed her teeth: evenly formed and close together—but yellow and shading to a darker coloration from neglect.

The odor of her breath, vented hard to power the curses, sent the flies into greater suicidal ecstasy. But Caroline ignored them and the heat now: screwing up the pages of the catalog in a tight fist, she whirled and ran back along the street to the padre's house. Her bare feet kicked up dust which rose lazily into the hot air and then drifted down again to blur the impressions of her footfalls. Some particles floated high enough to become pasted to her face, her chest, her breasts and her midriff. Her blonde hair, trailing out behind her in the

3

slipstream of her speed, became another shade darker as more dust clung to its greasy strands.

She scooped up the three-legged stool as she crossed the threshold of the house, and hurled it into a corner of the empty room as she slammed the door closed behind her. Without shortening her stride she went up the staircase two treads at a time, along the landing and through the only open doorway. When she emerged she was gripping a brass-framed Winchester .44 and her sneer had been transformed into a grin—a sour grin that exposed her discolored teeth to a greater extent. She moved more slowly now, the heavy breathing of exertion rasping in her throat. Midway along the landing there was a ladder with two missing rungs sloping up through a trap door into the attic. After hurling the rifle up into the opening, she climbed the ladder. Clumsily.

The dry heat under the roof of the house was more uncomfortable than out on the street but she took the time to refasten her dress from the waist to the top of the bodice before she picked up the rifle and stepped across the joists to the front pitch.

Like all the other stone- and timber-built houses and business premises in Rain, this one had a tiled roof. The fact that this one had more holes than most—she had removed many tiles the day after she arrived—was hardly noticeable.

Sometimes standing erect, and at others in varying degrees of a crouch, she moved from one hole to another: her green eyes now gleaming with a light of excited expectation as she tracked the approach of the wagon towards town.

It was a simple and aged buckboard, its timbers warped and cracked and its metalwork rusted. There

4

were two gray draft horses in the traces and a gray-haired man up on the seat. He was an ugly old man with warts on his bulbous nose: the flaccid skin hung on his thin face, deeply lined to show that his soured expression was a virtually permanent fixture. His jaw moved regularly as he chewed on a plug of tobacco and his bristled chin was stained yellow by the spilled juice.

He had failed to see the girl who advanced almost to the western end of Rain's street before she whirled and raced back into hiding; for his eyes had been dimmed by age for many years. Over such a distance, the town appeared to him as no more than a dark colored smudge on the gray and dusty landscape. Nor did he attempt to define solid shapes against the indistinct blur. For he had been to Rain many times in the long ago and had no reason to believe it was again inhabited by any living thing except wild animals and insects. So he merely gazed morosely at a point midway between the swaying heads of the two horses as he chewed on the tobacco and smelled the cloying sweetness of old death on the hot air.

He had known Rain when it had been a fine town, built by good but misguided people who put their trust in faith rather than truth.

Rain was a broad street, four hundred feet long, on an east-west trail between the Trinity and Red Rivers, in scrub desert country where only cactus and patches of tough grass grew. One side of the street was shaded at midday by the mesa which reared a sheer cliff a hundred and fifty feet skywards to the south. But, for most of the day, the entire town was exposed to the cruel glare and heat of the sun.

The two-story houses and stores, were built of the finest materials which had been hauled in over many miles from the east. A church and a meeting hall were constructed of smooth black marble shipped across the ocean from Europe.

No saloon or dance hall or restaurant. Rain had never been planned as that kind of town—nor as an attraction to the kind of people who desired such inessential luxuries. The drovers, for instance, who herded Texas cattle to Kansas up the Western Trail far out to one side of town or the Chisholm Trail even further away to the east.

"Crazy waste of good money," the old man growled as he hauled on the reins and kicked over the brake lever, bringing the buckboard to a halt at a midway point on the street. It was just about ten o'clock and the only shade in town was provided by the buildings themselves.

Familiar with discomfort, the old man sought no other shade except for that provided by the broad brim of his much dented, sweat-stained ten-gallon hat He did not look around as he hitched the reins to the brake lever and climbed down off the seat, wincing as age-stiffened joints protested the activity after a long ride.

Up under the roof of the padre's house, Caroline Keyes had already suffered disappointment and anger after the letdown of seeing the old man she did not know. Then there had been fear for a few moments—as she checked the country to the north and east of Rain through other holes in the tiles. But the appearance of the old-timer aboard the wagon was no part of a trick for nothing moved out on the desert. So, after raking her eyes along the ragged top edge of the mesa which blocked the southern approach to town, she became calm and viewed the newcomer with idle curiosity.

She was too familiar with the rancid smell of her own unwashed body to be aware of its stink any more. Thus, she did not know that this odor was masking the more evil one of death which the old man had brought to Rain—until he drew the burlap cover off the bed of the wagon and she saw the two corpses.

The old man almost died then. For Caroline vented an involuntary gasp of horror, loud enough, she was sure, to be heard from one end of the street to the other. So certain, she thrust the barrel of the yellow-boy Winchester through the hole and drew a bead on the stooped back of the man.

But his hearing was more badly affected by age than his vision. He heard just the crackle of wax against his eardrums as he leaned into the rear of the buckboard and grasped two ankles. Then he stepped backwards and straightened, hauling both corpses from the wagon at the same time.

The girl withdrew the rifle barrel and blinked the sweat of tension from her eyelashes as she leaned closer to the hole. She shuddered as the shoulder-blades of the face-upwards corpses came clear of the buckboard and the weight of the bodies dragged their heads off the timber. The old man released his hold on the ankles and the bodies slammed to the ground.

Dust exploded upwards, then floated down again. The old man spat a long stream of yellow-stained saliva far to the side and rubbed his palms on his shirt.

Caroline stared at the corpses. Both were youngsters in her own age group, dressed in check shirts, black denim pants and scuffed riding boots, one with a kerchief at his neck, the other without. Both wore gunbelts, with no bullets in the loops nor guns in the holsters. Each with a bullet hole in his belly, the fabric of the shirts crusted with congealed blood over a wide area. Other dried blood showed at the stumps of their wrists where their hands had been hacked off.

7

By the time the girl was able to tear her horrified gaze away from the two mutilated corpses, the old man had flung the burlap sheet on to the rear of the buckboard and climbed back up on to the seat.

Now he took up the reins, kicked off the brake lever and quietly spoke the horses into making a slow, wide turn on the broad street between the padre's house and the meeting hall. The rims of the wagon wheels cut deep ruts into the powdery dust, impressed here and there across the footprints made by the girl—who was abruptly tense with fear again as the old man halted the team. She clenched her fists tighter around the frame and stock of the Winchester, her knuckles showing white through the ingrained dirt but she did not bring the rifle to the aim.

The man on the wagon immediately below her had stopped simply to delve a bony hand into a pocket of his patched shirt. He drew out a tight-packed plug of tobacco and spat the chewed piece on to the street before biting off a fresh chunk.

Then he looked, squint-eyed, around the town for the first time since his arrival, sourly and without suspicion. "Yeah," he growled. "Sure was one crazy waste of good money." Suddenly he grinned, the expression revealing his toothless gums and making his loose-skinned face even uglier. "But folks that got money are entitled to spend it any which ways they please."

He had turned his head to address the lifeless faces of the dead men. "And I sure am glad that guy was willin' to ante up fifty bucks apiece for me to haul you two stiffs out here."

Caroline was immediately deeply interested in what the old-timer was saying. But there was little more to hear. For he had set the team moving again, heading back out for the west trail over which he had come. He

8

swung his head around and vented a cackle of cracked laughter as he took a final look at the corpses, slumped and stiff in the harsh glare of the bright sunlight.

"Ain't no mourners for you stiffs!" he yelled gleefully. "But at fifty bucks apiece I guess you can reckon yourselves a couple of the dear departed."

# CHAPTER TWO

"Don't suppose you're drummin' for a patent medicine company, young man?" Flora Porter asked, grimacing and clenching her fists as the off-side wheels of the stage lurched across another pothole in the trail.

"No, ma'am," Adam Steele told the woman.

"My Ma always said there was no patent medicine that'd ever be invented to cure old age," Joanne Brady said dully. Then snapped her head around and gasped as she wiped the expression of boredom off her face. "Oh, I'm sorry," she went on hurriedly. "To speak of a lady's age in such a way is not polite. I . . ."

Mrs. Porter showed a pained smile which hinted at the beauty she had possessed before time had put close to seventy years behind her. "Never mind, my dear," she assured. "Enjoy your youth while you have it—and all that goes with it. Includin' the privilege of sayin' the wrong things at the wrong time without appearin' crass."

The twenty-year-old girl smiled her relief and returned to her disinterested contemplation of the Texas terrain which spread to infinity beyond the window. She was in the left corner seat, facing forward. Mrs. Porter was at the other end of the same seat. Both women had wedged valises and carpetbags between

11

themselves to provide some sort of support on the bumpy, swaying ride.

Adam Steele sat in the center of the opposite seat, legs apart and braced on the floor with his back pressed hard against the thinly padded rest. His right hand was curled over the edge of the seat; his left was fisted loosely around the frame and cylinder of a Colt Hartford revolving rifle to hold it lengthwise along the seat.

"But you do sell somethin', I'm sure of that," Mrs. Porter went on, looking intently at the Virginian. "Of course, the girl is absolutely right. Nothin' will ever cure the discomfort of muscles past their prime. But a drink of the right kind of colored water can work wonders if the mind is willin' to believe."

Steele acknowledged the comment with a slight nod of his head, and continued to gaze at a pencil drawing of a river scene framed behind cracked glass above the seat opposite him.

"Then again," the little old lady with aching joints continued, "sometimes a little nip of somethin' stronger than colored water can be even better. It wouldn't happen to be liquor you travel in, would it, young man?"

Steele pursed his lips, but in no way did this indicate he was losing patience with the talkative Flora Porter. For his tone remained even. "The only thing I sell, ma'am, is my skill."

The old lady was suddenly excited. Even when the stage lurched across a whole series of potholes, she did not flinch nor allow her bright smile of anticipation to waver. "Medical skills?"

The Virginian shook his head. "They're for keeping folks alive, ma'am. Mostly I kill people."

Mrs. Porter allowed her mouth to fall open, but uttered no sound. The girl snapped her head around again, and vented a low-pitched shriek.

12

Steele smiled gently at each in turn. "Relax ladies," he soothed. "Only when I'm working and when I have to. Right now I'm on vacation."

He returned to his study of the framed drawing, conscious that the women were still staring at him as their shock lessened into disbelief.

It was probable that neither of them had ever seen a self-confessed killer in the flesh at close quarters. And, if they had ever conjured up in their imaginations what such a man should look like, the mental pictures would surely never have come close to resembling the soft-spoken Virginian sharing this stage trip with them.

He was small of stature and slight of build: standing about five and a half feet tall and weighing no more than a hundred and sixty pounds. There was physical strength at his command though—they could see this now, as they studied him closely for the first time since he boarded the stage at a way station ten miles back down the trail. It was visible in his ungloved hands and the easy way in which he supported himself to remain casually upright on the seat despite the pitch and roll of the fast moving stage.

But what of his character and its strength? His face gave away nothing about this. It was a commonplace countenance with a nondescript handsomeness in the set of the features. Lean, clean-shaven and bronzed by exposure to weather. Scored around the coal-black eyes and the gentle mouthline by the passage of some thirty-five years or so. Yet at first glance he had seemed older, undoubtedly because of his prematurely grey hair which he wore cut short—with the long sideburns neatly trimmed. Again, when he smiled, there was suddenly a certain boyishness which made him appear much younger.

His clothing was city style, obviously expensive but

now the worse for wear. A grey suit with blue stitching, a purple vest and a lace-trimmed white shirt. Riding boots in two-tone brown and white. A grey Stetson which he had not taken off but which he had touched deferentially on boarding the coach and seeing the women. And a kerchief of grey silk which hung around his neck, unknotted.

The experienced eyes of the widowed Mrs. Porter drew much from the cut and condition of Steel's clothing. She judged him to be a man with inclinations toward stylish living, but fallen upon hard times, and having to make the best he could from what he had. For, although stained and even torn here and there, the clothes had been brushed free of dust. As for the man wearing the dudish clothing, his hands and face were clean and he had shaved that morning. And his teeth gleamed untarnished white when he smiled.

The innocent eyes of Joanne Brady saw the same clues to one aspect of the Virginian's character but failed to draw any conclusions from them. Because her mind was entirely concerned with a subject vastly more important to her—the shameful responses she felt stirring deep within her body as she adjusted to being in close proximity to a man who killed others for a living.

"Well, I'm very pleased to hear that," Mrs. Porter said with a nervous laugh. "For I declare I'm happy to suffer the rheumatics if the alternative is kill or cure."

She laughed again, then covered her small mouth with a thin hand as she recognized the shrill tone for what it was.

Steele was irritated at himself and felt sympathy for the frightened old lady. He showed her his boyish smile and even managed to inject some warmth into his dark eyes. "Mostly, I was kidding, ma'am," he assured.

But she was looking out of the window on her side of

the stage, seeing nothing as she patted her sweat-sheened face with a lace-edged handkerchief. If she heard him, she chose to ignore him.

She was in her late sixties, with a girlishly slender body clad in a plain grey dress. Her hat was anything but plain—brimless and set at a jaunty angle on her severely-styled white hair, with small bunches of multi-colored imitation flowers sewn around the crown. Below this, her once beautiful face was pale and lined, with just a faint patch of red rouge on each sunken cheek. Her eyes were bright blue, clear and intelligent looking.

"I don't believe you, sir," Joanne Brady said softly.

Like Mrs. Porter, she chose to pretend that something of great interest outside the speeding stage held her attention.

"It's not important, Miss Brady," Steele replied. Then added softly: "To you."

The girl's fear expanded again. "How do you know my name?"

"Stage driving is a lonely job," the Virginian answered evenly, his drawling voice betraying his origins as clearly as if he had never left his native state until that morning. "Hard to keep the talkative ones quiet when they find a willing listener."

"Oh," the girl exclaimed, calm once more.

She was still overweight with the puppy fat of youth. About two inches taller than Steele, she had large breasts, a thick waist and broad hips. Her dull green jacket and long skirt fitted too snugly, emphasizing the too-generous curves of her body. Her hair was a rich brown, arranged in two pigtails, the ends of which brushed her broad shoulders.

Just as the old lady's features hinted at lost beauty, the lines of the girl's face promised a similar brand of

15

beauty which would be revealed once the fleshiness was gone and when she had outgrown the mass of red pimples she now tried to conceal beneath a heavy layer of cream and powder. Her sole attractive feature at present was a pair of large brown eyes in a frame of long lashes.

"I think we should be grateful, my dear," Mrs. Porter said suddenly aftter a long pause during which only the thud of hooves, the clatter of wheels and the creak of straining timber had disturbed the hot Texas silence. "We are in wild country where just about anythin' could happen to mere women with only a garrulous stage driver between them and danger."

"I think so, too," the girl agreed.

Both of them looked toward Steele again. But now he seemed to be lost in concentration on the framed pencil drawing.

"Did you hear what we said, young man?" Mrs. Porter asked, her tone more insistent. "Joanne and I are most pleased to have your company on this trip."

"Either of you rich?"

The old lady blinked.

The girl was confused by the query.

Steele glanced briefly at each in turn, with coal-black eyes that seemed incapable of ever expressing even the mildest degree of warmth.

"What I sell comes higher than patent medicine and doctoring," he said to the picture. "Real high when I'm on vacation."

Mrs. Porter grimaced, her look of scorn far more deeply etched into her thin face than when she reacted to pain. Joanne suffered fear again. And, behind this, another shamefully pleasurable stirring of an emotion she only partially understood.

The stage slackened its speed as the driver pulled his

16

team out of a gallop. The two women, still responding to the harshness of Steele's attitude, were unconcerned with anything else. But the Virginian was constantly aware of his surroundings, alert to any minor change which could signal a threat. Thus, he immediately snapped out of his morosely contemplative mood.

The drop in speed had been too sudden, lacking the skilled smoothness with which the driver had previously handled his team. A gallop, a canter, a trot and a walk, with brake blocks squealing against wheels—hard and long enough to generate heat and produce the acrid taint of smoke.

"Stay calm, folks!" the driver yelled as soon as the stage had jolted to a halt. "Could be nothin' to worry about!"

He sounded as anxious as the women looked as they half rose from their seats to peer out of the door's open windows.

Steele's only moves were slight—to reach into a pocket of his suit jacket, take out a pair of buckskin gloves and pull them on to his hands. He had started to do this the moment he sensed the haste of panic in the driver's actions. His fingers interlocked to push the buckskin tight between them as the driver started his unconvincing entreaty.

"No trouble, mister!" another man called. "We just need a ride."

"Thank goodness," Mrs. Porter sighed, flopping back on to her seat and mopping at the sweat on her brow again.

"Oh," Joanne breathed.

Steele placed one hand on his right knee and the other became fisted around the Colt Hartford again. He swung his head to left and right.

The stalled stage was in a narrow ravine with the debris of ancient rock falls littering the floor at the foot of high cliffs. Four men were standing on large boulders, two on either side of the stage. Men in gray Stetsons, checked shirts, and gray denim pants with faces made gray by the dust clinging to sweat and bristles. Each had a big Colt .45 jutting from his tied-down holster—and held a Winchester slantwise across the front of his body.

Four ridden-out horses were standing behind the two men on Steele's left. Old sweat lather was drying white on the coats of the animals. Their eyes were large and bulging and their nostrils were flared as they sought to suck in more of the hot air than their lungs could accommodate. Their heads hung low and they did not even have the energy to swish their tails at the flies which attacked them. Their saddles had been removed but they were still bridled, with the reins loosely knotted to make each a prisoner of the other three. The two with their flanks turned towards the stage displayed the blood-run ugliness of wounds caused by cruelly used spurs.

"Sure, fellers," the driver replied with enthusiasm which failed to mask his fear. "Come aboard and welcome. One'll have to ride on top, though."

"No hardship," the spokesmen for the quartet said. "Much obliged."

All four jumped down from the boulders, stooped to gather up their saddles, and advanced on the stage. They held their Winchesters one-handed now, low down, but kept their thumbs hooked to the hammers.

Steele moved his own rifle down between his knees, the stockplate resting on the floor.

"It's going to be all right, isn't it?" Joanne whispered as the stage rocked and creaked while the saddles were hurled up on to the roof and one of the men climbed aloft.

18

"I just have the one quarrel with them," Steele replied.

Both doors were swung open and the two women made to stand and shift their hand baggage from the seat to the rack above them.

"Now, now, ladies. We'll do that for you." When the man grinned, his teeth showed very white against his dirty face. "Billy, Pat. Get them bags shifted."

He was the eldest of the group. About forty, with a beefy build and a round face with bulbous cheeks and a broad mouth.

"Sure, Al. Howdy, ladies. Me and Pat'll be happy."

Billy was no more than twenty. A match for the older man's six foot height. But thin enough for the contours of his ribs to show through the tight fit of his shirt. His grin revealed crooked teeth, with gaps where two were missing.

Pat didn't smile as he came in through the opposite door and began to help with moving the baggage. He was thirty, give or take a year, with a squarish head and features and a complexion mottled by freckles. His build was short and squat with no waist. He did not alter his sullen expression as he dropped into the seat opposite Mrs. Porter. Merely sighed softly as he banged the door shut.

"There, ain't this cozy?" Billy asked rhetorically as he took the seat facing Joanne, his grin taking on a leering edge as he stared blatantly at the fabric of her jacket stretched tight over her large breasts.

"Keep your mind on what's at Rain, Billy," the leader of the bunch growled with menace as he climbed aboard, pulled the door closed behind him and sat between the two women, facing Steele. Like the other men he rested the stockplate of his Winchester on his left knee, gripping it around the frame with the muzzle al-

19

most touching the roof. His right hand lay on his groin, only inches from the butt of his Colt.

"Sorry, fellers!" the driver called. "Only can take you to the trail fork five miles ahead. We swing south for Fort Worth there."

He gasped then, and there was more fear in the sound than if he had vented a shrill scream. Then came the unmistakable sounds of a revolver hammer being cocked and the cylinder turned.

"Figure to change your route is all, mister," the new passenger outside the stage said. "But we can change the driver if that's the way it has to be."

Inside, only the oldest man drew his Colt. He was cramped by the women either side of him and the seat back. But still he was fast. Elegance was unimportant. He showed the whiteness of his teeth in a snarl as he drew a bead on the center of Steele's chest. "Heard you say you got a quarrel with us, dude," he rasped between the clenched teeth. "You wanna tell me what it is? So we can settle it here and now?"

"Ready to roll, Al?" the man on top called.

"A minute or less, John," Al answered, not shifting his gaze from Steele's face.

"The way you've been riding those horses it looks like you haven't got that long to waste, feller," the Virginian said, glancing out the window at the four sorry looking geldings.

Pat continued to stare sullenly down at his hand fisted around the Winchester frame. Billy grinned eagerly at Steele's profile. Both women were rigid with fear, gazes transfixed on the aimed gun.

"Rode 'em hard sure enough," Al supplied. "Last couple of miles was the worse for 'em. On account of we needed fresh mounts and knew the stage was scheduled through here."

"Why you did it doesn't interest me, feller," Steele told him. "It's done. So are the horses."

"You're breakin' my heart, dude."

"He's right, Al," Pat said dully. "We oughta put the nags outta their misery. Even if we turned 'em loose they'd die of thirst in this country."

"You got lead to waste on 'em?" Al sneered.

Pat shrugged, still gazing at his own hand. "Guess not."

"None of us have, dude. But if you figure you can take care of it from here, take care of it."

The Virginian nodded and eased the Colt Hartford up from between his knees. The revolver continued to be trained on his chest. Al backed the tacit threat with a spoken one.

"But don't get any ideas about shootin' anythin' exceptin' horses, uh?"

"Like I said to the ladies, I'm on vacation," Steele answered.

The three men eyed him quizzically as the two women screwed their eyes tight shut and pressed their hands over their ears. Steele rested his cheek against the rifle stock and cocked the hammer as he aimed out through the window.

The four shots came close together, the acrid taint of exploded powder serving to mask for a few moments the stink of the three newcomers' sweating bodies.

Billy watched the geldings die, each animal issuing a gush of blood from between its eyes as its front legs crumpled and it rolled over on to its side. He grinned.

Pat lost interest in his own hand and licked his thick lips in admiration as he watched the skill with which the Virginian fired. The smoothness of the hammer being cocked and the way the trigger was squeezed. The ease of the ride with the recoil and the calmness of the aim being adjusted to take the animals' rearing and flailing panic into account as their number diminished.

Al read the lettering inscribed into the gold plate screwed to the side of the Colt Hartford's fire-charred stock:

TO BENJAMIN P. STEELE, WITH GRATITUDE— ABRAHAM LINCOLN.

"You should have took in a play one night the other year," Al growled wryly as Steele grunted his satisfaction with the slaughter and replaced the still smoking rifle between his knees. "Man who can shoot as good as you might have saved a grateful friend." He raised his voice as he nodded towards the Colt Hartford. "Let's move it, John."

The driver yelled to his team, let off the brake and cracked the whip. The stage jerked into motion and Mrs. Porter and Joanne opened their eyes and uncovered their ears.

"Rifle was given to my father," Steele answered. "I inherited it."

It was obvious Al didn't like to be wrong. He grimaced as he pushed the revolver back into its holster— but kept his hand draped over the butt. "Keep ridin' easy, dude, and maybe it'll be a long time before your next-of-kin gets to inherit it."

The old lady made a sound of disgust deep down in her throat.

"You say somethin', ma'am?" Al asked.

The stage was making steady progress up an incline out of the ravine. Pat was back studying his fisted hand. Billy stole surreptitious looks at Joanne Brady's bosom. Al studied Steele and the Virginian gave the impression he was willing to allow the motion of the moving stage to rock him into easy sleep.

"I didn't, but I will!" Mrs. Porter answered emphatically, with a glare towards Steele. "I'd say you have no need to worry about that young man! The kind that boasts of killin' men and then shoots down innocent beasts!"

"Mrs. Porter!" the girl exclaimed, her voice shrill with nervousness.

"Forget it, sweetheart," Al assured Joanne without looking at her. "Gunslingers come in all shapes and sizes. Soon as I saw the way he handled the fancy piece, I knew what he was. But his quarrel with us is finished now. Right, dude?"

He raised his voice for the final two words.

Steele cracked open his eyes. "Right, feller," he replied wearily.

"And you do not care that we are to be taken miles away from our destination?" Mrs. Porter insisted vehemently. "By force of arms!"

"No, ma'am," the Virginian replied, closing his eyes again.

She made another sound of disgust. "And to think I once said Joanne and I were pleased to have you along with us. Some protector you turned out to be!"

"He never promised anything!" Joanne argued.

"Nor did anythin'! Even to help himself! To my mind he is nothin' more than a coward! Pretendin' he has no objection to bein' taken . . ."

"There was nothing he could do!" the younger woman cut in, her anger rising to the same level as that of the old lady.

"Without gettin' himself killed," Al agreed evenly. Then he laughed. "Hey, Steele! How's it feel to have a little girl built like this one fightin' for you?"

23

Joanne's pimples became almost invisible as she blushed scarlet under the thick make-up. "He means nothing to me!" she blurted. "It's just that I can understand why he was unable to . . ."

"You don't wanna believe that crap, Steele," Al interrupted. "I figure all you gotta do is say the word and she'll do anythin' you want her to." He laughed harshly.

"I've never . . ." the girl started, but found the words drowned by a rising tide of choking embarrassment.

"Always gotta be a first time!" the grinning Billy said with a guffaw.

"What you figure, dude?" Al asked, his tone hardening.

Steele pursed his lips and opened his eyes. He looked around the faces of his fellow passengers and saw that Mrs. Porter had become as morose and withdrawn as the man seated opposite her; that Joanne was on the verge of tears as her shame reached towards painful proportions; and that Al and Billy were ready to inject a strain of cruelty into their humor.

He showed his boyish smile to the girl, who drew some assurance from the expression. Until he spoke. "I reckon I don't have any chance of sleeping with her," he said, and saw her scarlet blush shade almost to purple. "On account of all this talk," he added, leaning his head back and closing his eyes as his hat brim was pushed down over his forehead. "But I'm ready to give it another try."

# CHAPTER THREE

Al laughed, and there was only humor in the sound. Billy tried to imitate the older man, but his laughter rang with a false note. And Steele knew the youngster who had been eager for him to be prodded into retaliation against the taunts—was trying to hide his disappointment that Al had decided to withdraw from the dangerous game.

There was no more talk for a long time after the laughter ended: as the progress of the stage across northern Texas fell into the same pattern as before the halt in the ravine. Sometimes fast, then easy, occasionally no more than walking pace. The speed was dictated either by the terrain over which the trail ran or the need to conserve the strength of the team.

Seated between Billy and Pat, Steele was more comfortable than he had been before the unscheduled stop, with no need to exert himself to remain upright as the stage rolled and pitched and jolted. And, had he been enjoying greater peace of mind, he might have allowed himself to drift into sleep.

Instead, he returned to reflecting on the same train of thought which had occupied him before the two women tried to start a conversation with him—a train set rolling by the picture opposite him. And, as the memories

25

of a river trip crowded into his mind again, so the same bad taste seemed to turn the saliva rancid in his mouth.

It had been a bad time on the Mississippi and the Red, doing a job he didn't want simply because of the money, which he did. It was the first time he had ever allowed that to happen to him since that fateful April night so many years ago, but he had got something useful out of it besides money—a firm resolve never to allow such a thing again.

What he had done was to sacrifice his freedom. And freedom was one of the few precious possessions left to Adam Steele.

Long ago he had been able to have whatever he needed—or even thought he needed. He had enjoyed peace and plenty as the son of one of Virginia's richest plantation owners. But he had used his wealth and position wisely. Among his harmless pleasures had been shooting for game and breeding top class horseflesh. Thus he had realized his skill as a rifleman, and developed a feel for horses which he had just revealed to the other people aboard the stage.

Such skill and knowledge had served him well during the War Between the States when, as a cavalry lieutenant, he had been forced to hone them and learn more, first fighting for victory and then simply for personal survival.

The war had been a bad time, too, made worse by the fact that he had elected to wear Confederate gray while his father chose to support the Union cause. And, after making this decision, the young Adam Steele had surrendered his freedom for the first time. For a junior officer had to accept orders from higher authority, and carry the responsibility of the men under his command.

But there had been a cause and a burning belief in it which excused much; until the callow youth was forged into a man amid the death and destruction of a war in which there was no glory—and came to realize how hollow mere dreams could be.

Then the war ended, and Adam Steele was eager to savor peace and freedom, to forget all that he had seen while he was a prisoner in a chain of command—and much that he had learned. Most of all, he looked forward to a reconciliation with his father.

But, on the night Lincoln was shot in a Washington theater another man died—in a barroom right across the street. Lynched from a ceiling beam simply because he happened to be in the wrong place at the wrong time.

That man was Benjamin P. Steele. And, when that man's son discovered the hanging corpse and cut it down, the violent peace had begun.

Had there been freedom of choice for Adam Steele that night, and every day and night that followed until every man responsible for his father's cruel death was also dead? Perhaps not, but it was immaterial. He tracked the killers relentlessly from the east into the west, driving himself by a not-to-be-denied thirst for vengeance. His instruments of death were the weapons of war and those acquired on the bitter trail. The ultimate weapon was always the Colt Hartford rifle which was his sole material inheritance from his father, its stock blackened by the fire which had ravaged the plantation and razed the big house.

It had seemed to be over when the last of the lynch mob died—that was in Texas, too. But the law could not allow it to end that way, for personal vengeance was not an acceptable cause without a declared state of war and a uniform to justify it.

Steele was captured by the law, but escaped statutory punishment—protecting his freedom, and perhaps even

27

his life, by committing murder. Which forced him to endure a worse punishment: The law officer who died at his hand was Deputy Jim Bishop, his best friend since childhood days.

"Hey, Al!"

"Yeah, John?"

"You figure that's the place up ahead?"

"That's Rain, mister," the stage driver said. "And just why you wanna get to that place beats me."

Steele opened his eyes and set his hat straight on his head. Billy was standing up, peering ahead through one door window. Mrs. Porter was half out of her seat to look at the town through the other one. Joanne Brady was gazing at the Virginian with something close to pity in her big, brown eyes. Al and Pat were also watching him, both with intent curiosity.

"You ain't been sleepin', dude, but it looked like you was havin' a nightmare," Al said.

Steele was irritated with himself again, as he felt the lines of his lean face reshape into impassiveness from the involuntary expression they had held while his mind had been reflecting on the distant and recent past. In his profession it could be fatal for a man to reveal his emotions to others.

"Never have been happy to be in Texas," the Virginian drawled, controlling his self-anger into a tight ball at the pit of his stomach.

"Know how you feel, Steele," Pat growled sourly, with a glance out through the dusty windows to either side of Billy's stooped thinness. "Hot as hell and a lot more empty."

Steele gazed briefly out of the windows on the other side of the stage as Mrs. Porter resumed her seat, using her soggy and discolored handkerchief to rub more sweat and dust from her pale and wrinkled face.

Far to the south there was a range of low hills made indistinct by the heat haze of noon. Between the high ground and the slow moving stage there was a vast plain of scrub grass and tumbleweed and cactus with, here and there, a small outcrop of rock or a more substantial mesa. Nothing moved out there except the infrequent patches of shade, crawling inexorably into length as the blistering sun inched across its daily arc of cloudless sky.

"Folks who built Rain figured to turn this patch into a piece of heaven," the driver announced sourly. He spat forcefully down at the dust-layered trail between the rumps of the two closest horses.

"It's a friggin' ghost town, looks like!" Billy moaned, flopping back on to his seat and shaking his head. Dust which had caught in his curly black hair from beneath the clopping hooves of the team now scattered through the fetid air inside the coach.

He yelled in pain as Al lashed out a leg and kicked him hard on the ankle.

"What the . . . ?"

"Watch your language, Billy!" Al snarled. "We got ladies present."

"A foul mouth is the least of my concerns," Mrs. Porter said hoarsely.

Her age and the length of the trip through the hot morning were taking their toll of her. She was no longer sprightly and bright eyed. Weariness and pain made her face haggard and caused her slender frame to sag into the corner seat.

"Shut up, lady," Al said harshly. "And listen to the man topside."

The stage was moving at a crawl now as it ran into the hot shade of the high mesa's eastern end. The sounds of its motion were subdued and the driver did not have to shout to make himself heard as he readily accepted Al's invitation to talk.

"Bunch of queer speakin' religious folks from over in Europe. Kinda like the Mormons they got up at Salt Lake. Only these folks only allowed themselves the one wife each." He tried a laugh, but didn't like the sound of it and curtailed it. "One of the guys was the leader of the bunch. Kinda high priest who called himself the padre.

"Didn't have hardly no money when they lit on this piece of territory and marked out the town. But they sure had plenty of the foldin' stuff where they come from. Hauled in everythin' they needed to build the place. And ain't nowhere built so good outside of them big cities like New York and Chicago and San Francisco."

The passengers could see this for themselves now, as the stage rolled on to the broad street between the flanking buildings. They looked out of the windows and saw the dirt and neglect, the decay and the dilapidation, but all this just a surface first impression. It took only a little imagination to realize what the town had been like before it was abandoned.

Neat rows of substantially built houses, each standing in its own fenced garden with a flagstone walk from the front gate to the porch door. Here and there were even the withered skeletons of tinder dry saplings which had been planned to be shade trees.

Midway along the single street, where the driver brought the stage to rest, was the black marble church and the meeting hall next door. To either side of this, buildings with store fronts, each with a roofed sidewalk. Directly across the street was a house larger than all the others.

"That big place was where the padre lived," the

driver went on. "It's said the feller didn't want nothin' any better than the rest of the folks. But that they figured he deserved rewardin' for findin' this place." He spat again, aiming for a wad of dried up chewing tobacco in the dust. He missed. "They was all crazy with religion, that's plain to see."

Something else was plain to see, and the driver's tone of voice altered as he continued telling the story of the town. There was the tension of fear stringing his words together as the passengers stepped gratefully down from the halted stage.

"See how all the houses and other buildin's got sloped roofs with downpipes and water butts? Well, there ain't nothin' about this patch of north Texas makes it any different from other patches a hundred miles either way. But that padre feller, he reckoned he smelled rain in the air. Why he named the town what he did, I guess. And why it was built like a town where it rains most of the time."

Each passenger's prime concern after disembarking was to stretch cramped limbs. The two women continued to stamp their feet and bend and straighten their arms as the driver's voice became more and more tense. But the men had detected the change of tone, and searched out for themselves what had caused the sudden anxiety—the signs of the dust.

Hoofprints and wheel ruts, telling of a wagon's approach along the street, its turn and progress back the way it had come. The impressions of two pairs of feet—one pair booted and the other bare. And the telltale marks of where two weighty objects had been dragged from the center of the street to the church.

"But it didn't rain in Rain," the driver said quickly. And this time the laughter was involuntarily trapped in his throat so that only a choked gasp escaped. "And

31

they busted their ploughshares on ground near as hard as the marble they built the church with. Not one row of crop seed was ever planted."

"They just upped and left. Four years ago, I guess. Mexico, some folks say. Or further south, I figure. Down to some jungle country where it don't do much else but rain. People don't come here no more. Much . . . Oh Jesus!"

The women had recognized the signs of his fear now. And had halted their exercise to look around at the other men who all stood on one side of the stage, eyes raking the blank façades of buildings while their hands gripped tight to their rifles.

The shot which caused the driver to raise his voice in a shrill profanity came from inside the roof of the padre's house. And, as all but one pair of eyes swung to focus on the puff of white muzzle smoke at a small dark hole, Al muttered: "Frig it!"

Then, just for part of a second, all attention was directed at him. As he dropped his Winchester and fell hard to his knees. His head was bowed to stare at the lines of liquid crimson oozing up between the fingers of hands pressed to his bulging belly.

"And frig you, Hayes!" Caroline Keyes screamed, the abuse shrill to the very edge of hysteria.

"Hayes?" Pat breathed, just before Joanne screamed and a volley of rifle fire exploded.

And the stage driver cracked his team into movement.

Steele, Billy and John sent bullets cracking towards the hole in the roof from which the first shot had been fired. The girl in the loft triggered another from a hole six feet to the left of where she had violently announced her presence.

"Take cover, Joanne!" Mrs. Porter urged, gripping

the wrist of the screaming girl and dragging her into motion.

But the cover she intended to use was suddenly on the move—the four-horse team lunging into a gallop under the sting of the whip that raced the stage down the street.

"Get Al outta here!" Pat snarled, and dropped down on to one knee, his boot covering the hole in the ground dug by the second shot from the roof.

He started to fire at the roof.

Drifting dust hurled into the hot air by the headlong retreat of the stage draped a swirling curtain over the center of the street.

The sullen-faced Pat blasted bullets out of the insubstantial cover of grit, swinging his Winchester back and forth to rake the whole length of the sloping roof with a deadly hail of .44 caliber lead.

After the slaughter of the horses in the ravine and his first instinctive shot at the roof, Steele had only one bullet left in the Colt Hartford's cylinder. He whirled in a half crouch and took experimental aim, waiting for the dust to clear so that he could draw a bead on the back of the stage driver.

Billy and John had each taken hold of an arm of the injured man and were dragging him towards the meeting hall.

Steele got a fine view of the crouching back of the driver aboard the racing stage. And squeezed the trigger.

Joanne was fighting the old lady: in the grip of a mindless panic which made her believe everyone was her enemy while her screaming failed to mask the ceaseless explosions of rifle fire.

"You must, girl!"

"I won't! I won't. You're all trying to . . ."

33

The old lady ducked under a flying fist. And the wild blow, powered by the strength of terror, crashed into Steele's right wrist as he expended the last live bullet from the rifle's cylinder.

The barrel was wrenched on to a new line and the bullet angled across the street to smash a window of Rain's abandoned schoolhouse.

"The hell with you then!" Mrs. Porter snapped, as Caroline got another shot away from the roof, to dig up more dirt close to where the two women were struggling.

"Shit!" Steele rasped through teeth clenched in a silent snarl of rage.

He whirled, in time to see the old lady release the screaming girl and take off after Billy and John with their burden—hoisting the skirts of her dress so she was able to take longer strides. He also saw the girl fall on to her hands and knees and begin to beat at the ground with her fists. Then his eyes located the butt of the Colt jutting from Pat's holster.

He knew the stage was long out of revolver range. But not of Al's Winchester, which lay ten feet away with its frame stained by spilled blood.

Pat's rifle rattled empty as the final expended cartridge pinged on the barrel of the discarded weapon.

Steele lunged forward to claim the bloodied gun.

"Go get the bitchofabitchin' bitch, Pat!" Billy shrieked.

He and John rejoined the battle, exploding their rifles from the cover of the meeting hall porch as Mrs. Porter ducked between their barrels.

Pat was closer to the discarded Winchester than Steele. He merely had to release the empty rifle from his grip, lean to the side and grasp the unfired one. And he was racing towards the padre's house under the covering fire before Steele had made half the distance.

"The stage!" Steele yelled as he skidded to a halt and turned, snapping his head around to look from the retreating stage to the men in the porchway.

"We've done with it, dude!" John snarled.

Pat leaped over the picket fence and sprinted across the garden for the safety of the side of the house, disappearing from sight at the rear.

John said something to Billy and both men held their fire.

Joanne curtailed her screaming and beating at the ground and lifted her head to listen to the sudden silence which was broken only from afar—by the clatter of hooves and wheels.

Gunsmoke drifted, the strength of its acrid taint diminishing as it was neutralized by the hot, Texas air.

"Bastards! Bastards! Bastards!"

Caroline Keyes punctuated each repeated word with a rifle shot. From a single hole in the roof. Two of the bullets cracked close to Steele. The third smashed the heel off Joanne Brady's left shoe.

Terror became too great to bear and the girl pitched forward into a faint.

The Virginian whirled again, and went at a crouching run to the girl.

"Help them, you varmints!" Mrs. Porter shrieked. "Use your rifles!"

"We got us Pat to take care of, lady," John growled. He back-handed her across a thin cheek as she attempted to snatch his rifle from him.

She staggered back into the meeting hall.

Billy and John continued to peer intently at the holed roof of the padre's house across the street, raking their rifles from one end of it to the other.

With the empty Colt Hartford gripped in one gloved hand, Steele used the other to clutch an outstretched arm of the unconscious girl. Then he dragged her in from the center of the street.

Another shot was fired from the padre's house—the bullet chipping marble fragments from the meeting house porch. The two men ducked against the shower of stone and pumped off shots of their own.

Steele, his lean, bronzed, time-scored face set in an expression of strain that betrayed nothing of the rock-hard ball of anger inside him, altered course. He forced his legs into a run to haul his heavy burden over the final few feet and into the safety of the church's entrance porch.

He relinquished his hold on the girl and tilted the rifle upwards, turning the cylinder with a gloved thumb so that the spent cartridges dropped out and rattled on the marble flagstones beneath his feet.

The gloves fitted his hands skin-tight, not impeding his dexterity at all as he dug into a pocket of his suit jacket and took out fresh shells which he slid into the chambers.

The gloves were a relic of the War Between the States, which perhaps he had once worn to keep out the bitter cold on some eastern battlefield. He could not recall. Just as he could not remember what precise incident had caused him to come to regard the gloves as a lucky charm: paradoxically, because he set little store in the law of averages commonly called luck.

He was aware only that the wearing of the gloves—torn and scuffed and stained—was a matter of habit. He always donned them whenever he saw or sensed that a new outbreak of violence was about to encompass him, whether the warning be something like distant gunfire on a pitch-black night, or perhaps the way a stage slowed on a hot Texas morning.

After the final shell had been clicked into a chamber, there was silence. Then he heard his own and Joanne Brady's breathing. Time and space had swallowed up the sounds of the stage and he sighed his acceptance of the fact that he was too late to halt it.

He let the rifle become canted to his left shoulder and narrowed his eyes to peer across the sun-bright street at the padre's house. It was still and looked as deserted as every other building on the north side of the street. Only with hindsight was he able to see what made it different—the regularity, in height and breadth, of the row of holes along the pitch of the roof.

"How you doin', Pat?" Billy yelled, impatient and afraid.

"Shuddup, my stupid brother," John growled.

"I'm doin' friggin' lousy," Al rasped.

"Pat'll get her," John assured.

He was confident. The injured man was weak.

Steele pursed his lips and vented a low grunt of satisfaction as he felt the ball of rage become dissipated. He had survived and what was between the four men and the girl sharpshooter was not his concern. Unless he found himself caught in their crossfire again.

He lifted the latch and pushed open the big, brass-studded, solid oak door. The air inside the big church had been cooled by the marble of floor, walls and arched ceiling. Steele relished the way it flowed out around him, easing the sweat that sheened his face and pasted his clothing to his body.

Then he smelt the stench of old death as the heat from outside won the battle for control of the interior atmosphere. As his eyes adjusted from the glare of the street to the softer shafts of sunlight which were filtered through the stained glass windows he saw the corpses.

The two men with the holes in their bellies and no hands were propped into sitting positions, backs supported by the black marble altar so that they could gaze sightlessly down the length of the aisle to where Steele was silhouetted in the doorway.

Joanne Brady snapped open her eyes as she was jerked from unconsciousness. She tried to scream again as she stared through the Virginian's splayed legs and saw the ghastly tableau at the altar. But her vocal chords had been strained and she managed only a strangled gasp.

"Oh my God, what did I ever do to deserve this?" she wailed.

Steele cocked his head, listening to the hushed silence of the church. Then he sighed. "Something real bad, I reckon," he responded. "Seems you and He aren't on speaking terms."

# CHAPTER FOUR

The hot silence of the abandoned town was once more shattered by a rifle shot. But there was no sound of the bullet finding a target out on the street.

"I reckon that ends it," Steele said softly as he turned and looked down at Joanne Brady on the flagstones. Terror was etched more deeply than ever into the blemished surface of her fleshy face. But the calm tone and tranquil expression of the Virginian helped her to hold her emotions in check. "For now," he added.

"Pat?" Billy called, anxiety putting a whine into his voice.

"So kill me, why don't you?" This from the girl who had fired the first shot in the gun battle. Her words shrill, with anger rather than fear.

"You're too good to waste, sweetheart," Pat answered. "You wanna move that cute little ass down and out? So we can all see how the nooky's gettin' better?"

He was up under the roof of the padre's house, but did not have to shout to be heard by those emerging on to the street. Steele, with the Colt Hartford canted to his shoulder. Joanne hobbling on her broken shoe. John and Billy with their Winchesters still cocked and aimed. And Mrs. Porter, absently massaging the area of redness on her cheek where John had struck her.

"Friggin' make me!" Caroline snarled.

"Figure to, sweetheart . . ."

Billy guffawed.

". . . but you won't get no pleasure outta it if you got shattered kneecaps."

Two shots exploded in quick succession.

Caroline screamed.

Joanne turned and clung with both hands to Steele's arm. The Virginian was peering out to the west of town, watching as the stage swung off the trail to the south. Slow moving now. The driver taking care of his team for a wide sweep around Rain to pick up the trail to the east.

"All right! All right!" the girl surrendered.

"He'd have done it, you know that?" Billy said enthusiastically, bright eyes raking over the faces of Steele and the two women. "He'd have blasted her legs from under her and screwed the ass off her while she was still yellin'. He's a real mean bastard, that Pat Grant."

"Billy, I told you," Al groaned weakly from inside the meeting hall. "There's ladies present."

"Sorry, Al," Billy said quickly.

"Well, look at that, little brother," John muttered, and pursed his lips for a low whistle.

Steele was watching John. At close to thirty, he was about ten years older than Billy. Out of the same six-feet-tall, skinny mold. Maturity had added great strength of character to his hollow-eyed, sunken-cheeked face. The most evident family resemblance was in the teeth. They were as crooked as Billy's, but without gaps.

Now the Virginian joined the others in gazing across the street as the door of the padre's house swung open and the girl came out, trailed by Grant.

"I'm lookin', I'm lookin'!" Billy replied in high excitement.

Caroline's mutilated gown was still fully fastened from waist to the top of the bodice. But this left a great deal of flesh exposed and, where it did cover her, sweat pasted the fabric tight to her body to contour every rise and indentation.

"Disgustin'!" Mrs. Porter snapped.

"You're just jealous you won't never look like her again," John taunted.

Caroline swept her green-eyed gaze over all the faces turned towards her and treated them all to the identical look of contempt.

Steele tried to probe through the surface expression and the dirt to search out her true feelings. But she seemed genuinely unafraid—arrogantly resigned to her fate—as she kicked open the gate with a bare foot and swayed across the street ahead of Grant's levelled Winchester. She even emphasized the feminine motion of her hips and held her shoulders high so that her breasts thrust more firmly against the restraint of the dress silk.

"Damn it, Pat!" Billy yelled. "Let's strip that dress right off her right now."

He pushed his rifle towards his brother, who took it by reflex action. Then Billy started forward to meet the girl.

Her scorn expanded as it concentrated on the skinny youngster approaching her. "A beanpole like you'd slide right in and I wouldn't even know you was in there, sonny!" she taunted a boy no more than three years her junior.

"Why you smart mouth cu—" Billy started, snapping to a halt and reaching for his holstered Colt.

"Hold it, Billy!" Grant snarled, moving to the side to aim his rifle at the enraged youngster. "Al gets to talk to her before . . ."

"Man with a slug in his guts can't be boss no more, Pat," John interrupted.

The girl came to a halt, her arrogance evaporating like a globule of saliva on a hot stove lid. "Al?" she rasped, her green eyes widening as she looked at every face in turn again. Finishing up with her head screwed around to stare at Grant.

Grant was expressing a milder degree of surprise. Then his face gradually returned to its usual sullen set as he spoke. "I'm Patrick Grant, sweetheart. The kid's Billy Swan. Feller who looks like him is his brother John. The dude, the old biddy and the fat nooky ain't important. Just took the wrong stage is all. Feller you put a hole in is Al Root."

He transferred his attention to the Swans. "Let's go see Al. He's the boss of this outfit long as he can talk loud enough to give the orders."

There was a dangerous glint in his dark eyes which was a more potent threat than the muzzle of his Winchester.

"I thought . . ." Caroline began, then shook her head violently, swinging her long, blonde hair from side to side. Then tears welled up in her eyes and spilled from the corners to course down her filthy cheeks.

"Yeah, sweetheart," Grant growled. "You thought he was Hayes Elliott. So let's go talk to Al about that."

"Leave it, little brother," John Swan ordered grimly. "Pat's right about one thing. She's gotta talk before she gets screwed and dead."

The younger Swan was still tense with anger from the girl's abuse. But he nodded his agreement, spun around and snatched his rifle from John's grasp as he swaggered by to go into the meeting hall. John waited until the now subdued Caroline Keyes and her captor had entered before moving.

"Private business," he growled towards Steele, Mrs. Porter and Joanne as he strolled over the threshold and kicked the door closed behind him.

With the men and their guns off the street, Joanne Brady considered it safe to release her grip on Steele's arm. She kicked off her ruined shoe, stood lop-sided for a moment, then stooped to take off the good one and hurl it away.

"We've got the varmints!" Mrs. Porter snarled harshly and softly, forgetting about the pain in her cheek as she set the heavily flowered hat squarely on her hair. "They left you your gun, young man. And you already showed us you can use it real good."

The Virginian pursed his lips. "You want me to go in there and shoot them all, ma'am?" he asked, running the back of a gloved hand over a half day's growth of bristles on his jaw.

"Damn right," she whispered, scowling at him for failing to keep his voice down. "As prisoners they'd still be a whole mess of trouble for us."

"Then what would we do, ma'am?" Steele posed wearily.

"Get out of this God-forsaken place, of course!"

"No!" Joanne countered, her voice high and loud. "I think we should stay here. The stage driver is sure to tell the authorities what has happened. Isn't that so, sir?"

Fear had not deserted her. She had merely managed to gain some kind of control of it. But it was still latent and potent—and the imploring look in her big brown eyes as she gazed at the Virginian was a pitiful plea for help to keep it in check.

"I reckon there's a fifty-fifty chance of that," he allowed.

Mrs. Porter snorted, and whirled to head for the

open door of the church. "Enjoy your vacation while you may! I intend to pray for help from the Lord! Since no mortal man is prepared to lift a finger to save us."

The door of the meeting hall swung open and Grant emerged, angrily sullen. The buzz of talk which had been audible while the door was closed now ceased.

"I wouldn't go in there, lady!"

Mrs. Porter came to an angry halt as the freckle-faced, squarely-built man lengthened his stride to beat her to the church porch. "Am I to be denied makin' my peace with my God before you varmints murder me?" she growled.

"Don't plan on murderin' no one, lady," Grant replied, peering down the length of the aisle towards the altar. "Unless there's no other choice." He spat into the church and stepped out of the porch, ignoring the angry Mrs. Porter to nod towards Steele. "You got the right attitude, dude. Just stick around and keep your head down if shootin' starts up again. Try anythin'—and that includes leavin' town—and you'll join them fellers."

He jerked a thumb over his shoulder as he moved away from the porch.

"You know them?" the Virginian asked.

"Names are Flint and Sullivan."

"Were."

A nod. "Yeah, were," he acknowledged, and went back into the meeting hall, using an elbow to swing the door closed.

"There are dead men in the church?" Mrs. Porter gasped.

"With their hands cut off," Joanne supplied dully.

The old lady brought her own hands up to her mouth. But there was just a dry sound in her scrawny throat.

"Is there nothin' we can do?" she rasped between her clenched false dentures. And in her eyes was the same kind of plea which the younger women had earlier directed towards Steele.

"Not for them, ma'am."

"For us! You know I mean for us! You're not a fool."

The Virginian nodded as he turned his back on the old woman before her pleading look was totally swamped by new fear-inspired anger. "That's right. And only a fool would work for no reward."

Steele's mercenary callousness got to Joanne Brady and her expression and tone were as bitter as those of Mrs. Porter as she hissed, "How much would it take for you to break off your vacation, Adam Steele?"

"Not much," he answered with a soured glance around the derelict buildings of the street and the arid terrain beyond. "To make this town the last resort."

# CHAPTER FIVE

The Virginian was not on vacation. But, having allowed himself in an unguarded moment to reveal his line of work to the women, he had attempted to withdraw behind a screen of light-heartedness. Then the appearance of Root, Grant and the Swan brothers had turned the joke sour before he could develop it.

In fact, Steele was simply drifting west again, after being as far in the east as he had ever been since he set out on the vengeance trail in pursuit of his father's killers.

New Orleans had been the place where his eastward drift had ended. And there had been women trouble of the worst kind in the city and the Delta country of the Mississippi's lower reaches.

He had gone there with the intention of raising money. That was the sole reason he ever went anywhere since he had ridden out of the squalid Mexican village in which he had tried to drown his remorse about Bish's death with hard liquor.

This time it should have been different though. He had a small stake which he hoped to build on at the poker tables of the plush hotels. But there had been a woman, which was nothing new. And deceit and violence and death—as he had known, deep down, that there would be.

So he had had to move on, as inevitably as the sun rose each morning and set each night. And he had been unable to resist the temptation of earning some money in the process of leaving Louisiana—by accepting advance payment for a job he knew little about.

Thus, for the first time since he had placed himself outside the law, did he become what he had told the women he was—a gun for hire.

As he stood now, at the schoolhouse window, broken by the misdirected bullet from his rifle, he grimaced as he considered the label he had attached to himself.

Outside, the single street of Rain was deserted. Everyone trapped in the town by the vast distances of waterless country on all sides had retreated into the shade. Caroline Keyes and the four men were still in the meeting hall. And Mrs. Porter and Joanne Brady had entered the padre's house.

It was an hour past noon and the glaring heat of the sun seemed to increase as its source began the decaying arc down the western dome of the sky.

Steele hated no one unless he had a personal reason, so he felt no repugnance against professional killers as a breed. But he had always fought shy of becoming one himself.

He had killed for money before—between the time Jim Bishop died and when he stepped aboard the *Queen of the River*. But only because he had to, in order to survive, as an adjunct to completing the job he had been hired to do.

Many might consider that had been the case on the trip up the Mississippi and Red to Twin Creeks. But Steele could not think of it so, because his allies had been professional gunmen. And that was what made the difference to Steele. He had used his guns alongside

48

professional killers against amateurs—for money. Against men who fought simply for a belief.

In a holocaust which marked the end of the job the odds had been evened. But this had not been enough to expunge Steele's sense of guilt—just as those countless days of drunken stupor in Mexico had failed to smother his remorse over Bish.

"Steele! You two women! You wanna come over here?"

It was Billy Swan, shouting from the porch of the meeting hall. His tone was too tough and there was a swagger of bravado as he stepped out into the sunlight and raked his hat-shaded gaze from the school to the padre's house and back again.

"Al figures you oughta know what this is all about!"

Steele had entered the building by the doorway. Now, he allowed the rifle to fall forward from his shoulder, so that its barrel smashed against the already broken pane. As more shards of glass fell from the frame—out into the play yard this time—the younger Swan powered down into a crouch and pumped the lever action of his Winchester as he brought it to the aim.

"He want to get us all as scared as you, kid?" Steele called, swinging a leg over the sill and stepping outside.

"You crazy bastard, I mighta killed you!" the youngster snarled, as he eased upright, his hands trembling.

"If I had held still long enough," Steele drawled, crossing the yard and swinging his leg up again, to step over the fence.

"Do we have to come?" Joanne Brady called nervously.

"Al?" Billy asked.

"It don't matter. They ain't no use to us." Root's voice sounded stronger.

"Forget it!" Billy yelled towards the padre's house as Steele neared him. "We already got all the nooky we need, I figure!"

Steele glanced at the big house across the street and saw the old and the young woman standing at an upstairs window. The way the bright sunlight struck the dusty panes made them look somehow clean and neat and tidy.

"Inside, dude!" Billy barked, his throat pulsing. "And remember, I got an itchy trigger finger."

"You're just one big irritation, kid," the Virginian countered, going ahead of the gesturing rifle into the meeting hall.

It was as long as the church across the alley next door, but not so wide or high-ceilinged. The black marble kept half its length just as cool. The people who had abandoned Rain had stripped the building of every item of furniture so that it was just a dusty, empty shell. Sunlight shafted through the west windows to bathe the front half of the hall with glare. But there was shade at the far end and that was where Al Root lay, his head propped up against the marble front of an elevated platform.

His shirt and undershirt had been removed to make a pad and bandage covering the bullet wound in his belly. The girl was squatting down beside him, staring in horror at the dark stain which had soaked up through the dressing.

Grant leaned against the front of the platform to one side, sullen faced. John Swan sat on the edge of the stage to the other side, eyeing the girl lustfully as her crouching posture stretched her gown tight over the curves of her body.

"You bought yourself into a mess of trouble when you paid for your stage ticket, Steele," Root rasped as the Virginian moved down the hall, his boot heels rapping on the marble floor.

Billy Swan remained at the front of the building, peering out of a window to the right of the door.

"Not as much as you're in for free, I reckon."

Root grinned, then it became a gritted-teeth grimace as a new stab of pain cut through his belly. "That sure ain't nothin' to quarrel about," he allowed.

He was a dying man. Beneath the dirt and bristles on his fleshy face, his complexion was as white as the skin of his naked torso above the blood-stained bandage. His eyes looked sunken and spittle ran from a corner of his mouth whenever he opened his lips. Although his voice was strong, it was costing him a great deal from his diminishing reserves of energy to keep it that way.

"You shouldn't be talkin'," the girl complained, and bit on the knuckles of a clenched fist.

"Shut your mouth, bitch!" John Swan snarled. "You're all through with talkin' with it!"

Root even managed to generate a lustful look of his own in his pain-narrowed eyes as he glanced fleetingly at the girl. "Yeah," he sighed. "Hayes was always talkin' about the ways you knew of usin' that pretty little mouth."

"She just spoke sense outta it, Al," Grant growled. "You should rest a while. I can tell Steele the score."

The fatally wounded man sighed again. Then nodded as he reached out a hand, bunched a hank of the girl's long hair in a fist, and tugged at it.

She winced as the strands tightened and she began to experience pain at the roots.

"Yeah, you go ahead, Pat," Root urged. Then: "You rest down here beside me, girl. I don't figure to hurt you none. That's John's pleasure. I like . . . ah, that's what I like."

The girl had submitted to his insistent pulling of her hair and the almost tender tone of his voice. Now she was stretched out beside him, her head leaning against the front of the platform in the same manner as his. And he had released her hair to drape his arm around her shoulders, his hand dipping inside the top of her dress to cup the mound of her right breast.

An expression of contentment had spread across his wan face. The girl continued to be silently terrified. Swan stared down at the couple, his eyes fixed upon the movement of the dress fabric caused by Root's kneading hand.

"Her name's Caroline Keyes, Steele," Grant said with morose weariness. "And she made a bad mistake."

"Shot the wrong man, I reckon."

"That's right. See, the way she tells it—and there ain't no reason not to believe her—she staked a guy named Hayes Elliott. Staked him in a big way while he was settin' up a plan to rob an express car up in Missouri.

"Damn fine plan it was," He continued, nodding and coming close to a smile as he recalled a pleasant memory. "Me and Al and Billy and John were in on it."

"And Arnie Flint and Bud Sullivan," Root put in, finding a smell in the girl's filthy hair to enjoy while he worked on her breast.

"Yeah, them two guys as well. All seven of us. Good friends and good at workin' with each other."

"You knew I was his woman!" Caroline blurted out, apparently completely unmoved by Root's fondling. "You said he talked about me a lot. That he was gonna marry me, even."

Grant nodded. "All true, sweetheart." Then to Steele: "We hit that train on the button and only one guy got himself killed. The expressman. We all got away without a scratch—and close to a hundred grand in hard cash. All of it nice easy-to-carry bills. But we was hunted by express company men, the Pinkertons, the local law. Even some Federal marshals. So we decided to stash the money and scatter."

"Hayes decided," John Swan growled, not breaking his concentration on the erotic movements under the girl's dress.

"Sure. But we all agreed. Al. Just like we all agreed to wait for Hayes to get a message to us. About where and when we'd all meet to divvy up."

"Rain's a good place for that," Steele drawled.

Grant had worked a lot of saliva into his mouth. He spat high and long down the center of the meeting hall. "Yeah," he agreed without enthusiasm, and scowled towards the skinny back of the younger Swan who was still keeping watch on the padre's house across the street. "But we had some trouble gettin' here. Billy shot a man in a jerkwater Arkansas town and it wasn't easy springin' him from jail."

"The dude don't wanna hear our life stories, Pat," John rasped.

"Don't see why we have to tell him anythin'!" Billy snarled from the far end of the building.

"Attend to you chore, son!" Root countered.

"Yes, sir." Subdued.

"Shoulda been here ten days ago," Grant went on with the story. "Reason we run them horses into the ground. And found out how well you could handle that fancy rifle of yours."

He had been staring down at the floor between his boots for a long time. Now he raised his head and gazed levelly into the Virginian's impassive eyes.

"Town has you fellers spooked?" Steele asked evenly.

"Just listen to the rest of it!" Root snapped, as the

elder Swan wrenched his attention away from the girl to glare angrily at Steele.

"This little sweetheart tells us she was ditched by Hayes." Grant said, talking faster now. "Up in Abilene. Says Hayes got himself a new woman and she heard them plannin' somethin'. Seems they fixed to go down to Mexico with the whole hundred grand. With a stop-over here in Rain to make sure they wouldn't have to keep lookin' over their shoulders while they were spendin' all that money."

"Good place for that, too," Steele put in.

Grant nodded towards the girl. "Says she didn't know where Hayes had stashed the money. So she wasn't in no position to do nothin' up in Abilene."

John Swan, having lost interest in vicarious sex, was becoming impatient. "So she high-tailed it down here and figured to blast Elliott and his new woman and get the money."

"To share with you!" Caroline blurted out, trying to sit up. She gasped in pain as Root's clawed fingers dug hard into her flesh, holding her down.

"What you said," the injured man allowed flatly.

"Said, too, she's been here more than ten days," Swan continued. "Had about given up on Elliott and his woman showin' until an old-timer hauled in the corpses this mornin'."

"You know him, ma'am?" Steele asked.

"Not from Adam."

The Virginian showed a wry grin. "Sure glad you didn't mistake me for somebody else."

"Old-timer wasn't part of our bunch, Steele," Root said. "Just doin' a job for Hayes, I figure. And the girl could be tellin' it like it was about blastin' me by mistake. On account of she never saw any of the bunch except Hayes."

"Shit on that, Al!" John Swan snarled. "Elliott's got your build is all. You don't look nothin' like him 'ceptin' for that."

"To you, now," Root answered, disenchanted with the feel of the girl's flesh and withdrawing his hand. He rested it on her naked shoulder. "But if we believe what she says, she's been here near two weeks. All alone. Fryin' in the daytime and freezin' at night. Couple of mouthfuls of water a day and hardly nothin' to eat. With somethin' more powerful than just thirst and hunger gnawin' at her insides."

"I guess I can go along with that, Al," Grant said sourly. "Sun was bright and she was more than a little crazy. She was expectin' to see Hayes and you coulda looked like him enough from where she was. Maybe she even figured the fat nooky for his new woman."

"Does that make the lead in your gut feel any better, Al?" John Swan asked with a brutal tone.

Root sighed. "Sure don't, John," he forced out between clenched teeth as his eyes became dulled by a fresh wave of agony. "You wanna give her a taste of what's comin' to her?"

Terror expanded inside Caroline Keyes. She gasped and tried to rise as the elder Swan pushed forward off the front of the platform. But Root's talon-like hand tightened its grip over her shoulder to hold her down.

Swan left his Winchester where it rested, so had both hands free to stoop and grasp the girl's naked ankles. "Don't fight me, girl," he warned hoarsely as Root released his grip on her so that she could be dragged away from him. " 'Cause there are hard times and hard times."

Her fear swelled to the extent of paralyzing her. Her arms trailed out helplessly above her head with her long hair between them as she was hauled over the marble floor, and she could not move when Swan halted and released her ankles. Her legs slapped uselessly to the floor, splayed in an enforced attitude of invitation. For she was naked to the waist now, the act of being dragged across the floor having hiked up the ragged skirt of her gown to where it fitted snugly.

The gaze of every man was drawn to her slender thighs, her flat belly and the dense growth of blonde hair with her gaped sex at its center.

"Attend to your chore, Billy!" Root repeated. "You'll get yours later."

"Damnit, John!" the youngster whined as his brother drew a knife from a sheath at the small of his back. "Don't mark her up too bad!"

"She'll be part of your pay, if you've a mind," Pat Grant said dully as John Swan crouched beside the unmoving girl and began to use his knife on the gown. "Kinda bonus, like. But what you'll really be workin' for is Hayes's share of the express money."

"He's that good, uh?" Steele asked as Swan completed slicing the dress from Caroline's body and flipped it apart to either side, so that the whole length of her was exposed to the eyes of the men.

Her right breast was bruised and scratched from where Root's fingers and nails had punished it. Elsewhere, her flesh was delineated with meandering lines formed by dust clinging to old sweat.

Only John Swan and Root were aroused by the girl's enforced nakedness. Steele and Grant watched coldly as they talked—while Swan drew new lines on the helpless flesh: the point of his knife sinking just deep enough to erupt blood.

"Hayes is real smart . . ."

One bloody circle around the right nipple.

". . . and ain't none of us four any great shakes at shootin'."

Another around the left nipple. The girl formed her mouth into a grimace as she experienced the smarting sensation of the broken skin.

"Hayes might show up alone or with his new woman. Or he might even have some new buddies. You seen this town and the mesa in back of it. Strong-handed or alone, men or a man could keep a whole friggin' army pinned down here."

Swan lay the knife on the floor and went into a kneel, leaning down to take the crest of the punished right breast in his mouth. He was gentle as he suckled on the warm, salty blood. But he did not swallow as he moved his lips to the left breast.

"One man could do that," Steele agreed. "If he was good with a rifle."

Swan's usually sunken cheeks were ballooned with blood-dyed saliva as he brought up his head.

"You're the only guy we've ever seen handle a rifle better than Hayes," Grant said.

Swan spat forcefully into Caroline's face from a height of three feet, spraying her from jaw to above her hairline. She trembled from her fingertips to her toes and clamped her eyes and lips tight closed, but uttered no sound of revulsion.

Anger became deeply etched into the thin face of Swan as he swung one knee up and forward, pivoting on the other so that he straddled her. Her mouth burst open under the force of expelled air as he slammed his rump down hard on her tortured breasts.

"Call me somethin', you two-bit whore!" he snarled, and cracked his right hand across her cheek.

She groaned.

The fingers of his left hand worked at unfastening the front of his pants.

"Use names, cow!" he demanded, spittle dripping from the corners of his mouth. And hit her again, swinging his arm in the opposite direction so that it was a backhanded blow to the other cheek.

She screamed.

"Words, cow! Words, whore! Call me names, bitch! So I can ram them back down your throat! Just like that bastard Elliott used to!"

"He never used to hurt . . ." the girl forced out, having to drag her speech from beneath the pressing weight of her sadistic tormentor.

"Hold it!" Root barked, as Swan groped inside the front of his open pants.

"He's markin' her up!" Billy whined.

Root's glinting-eyed lust was wiped away by glowering anger as he stared down the length of the meeting hall.

The younger Swan had turned his back on the window and advanced several feet away from it, aroused and eager for a close-up view of his brother's vicious assault on the girl.

Then terrified dismay took command of his features as he whirled and raced back to the window. Hearing, like all the other men, the beat of galloping hooves against the sun-baked Texas ground.

John Swan sprang up from his naked victim and lunged for his rifle on the platform. Grant was already running down the hall. Root draped a hand over his holstered Colt and grimaced with pain at the act of drawing the revolver.

Billy cursed his frustration at not being able to get a wide-angle view from the window, and wrenched open the door to run outside. He skidded to a dust-raising halt on the street.

"Not a move, girl!" Root growled, unable to do so himself. He aimed the Colt at her and thumbed back the hammer.

She froze for an instant. Then began to tremble again when the sound of thudding hooves rose as the horse raced on to the street. The noise triggered within her a greater degree of terror than any she had experienced since her capture.

"Fine, girl," Root rasped through gritted teeth, angered by his inability to do more than cover the helpless prisoner. "You just stay put."

Caroline's green eyes, with red spittle clinging to the lashes, searched the meeting hall and located Steele. She expressed a plea far more powerful than those which Mrs. Porter and Joanne Brady had directed towards him earlier.

"All you can do, ma'am," the Virginian told her softly as he turned his back on her to start along the hall. "Seems you're not going to get ahead."

# CHAPTER SIX

The racing horse drew level with the meeting hall and padre's house just as Steele emerged on to the street behind the Swans and Pat Grant.

Billy fired and cursed as he missed the sweat-lathered animal.

"Bastard!" Grant rasped, and started to bring his Winchester to the aim.

But another rifle cracked before the freckle-faced man had completed pumping the lever action.

The horse dropped in its tracks, its forelegs buckling and its head falling forward. Blood gushed from the hole where its bulging right eye had been and the horse died before it could snicker its pain. It's nose hit the rockhard ground under the layer of dust and the impetus of its gallop sent it into a high, ugly somersault. It crashed down on to its back with a sickening crack of breaking bone. And the force of the crushing horseflesh burst open the burden lashed to the saddle.

The burden was human—the scrawny, middle-aged man who had driven the stage into and out of Rain. He was almost in two pieces now, as the lifeless horse rolled on to its side hiding the man's legs but allowing his head and torso and arms to sprawl out in the dust. He had been dead before the ride back to Rain had started, the unmistakable exit hole of a heavy caliber bullet gaping at his throat. The crashing fall of the upside-down horse had caused an uglier wound, smashing his spine and pelvis and ripping open the skin of his belly.

Blood and liquids of colors other than red gushed from the pulpy insides of the man. Flies swarmed in to blot the ghastly mess with their black and iridescent bodies and wings.

But the four men had whirled away from the corpse and carcass before the flies settled, to run into the cover of the meeting hall and the church as a peal of harsh laughter filled the silence which followed the death of the horse. They crouched at marble corners, heads tilted back and moving from side to side, searching out the gleeful sharpshooter who had fired from the top of the mesa.

Then, abruptly, the sound was curtailed. And Steele was as confused as the others. For there had been an unnatural note to the laughter, unnerving not only because of its somehow ghoulish quality. There was also the fact that its source could not be pinpointed precisely on any single part of the bluff's high top. It had seemed to spill over the edge along its entire length.

"What the friggin' hell is happenin' out there?" Al Root demanded to end stretched seconds of tense stillness.

"Figure Hayes has showed up, Al!" Grant answered from one corner of the meeting hall's frontage.

"On a horse at full tilt, dammit?" the injured man snarled, his temper rising.

"That was his messenger, feller," Stelle supplied.

"What evil is takin' place in this town?" Mrs. Porter shrieked from the upstairs window of the padre's house.

The sun had shifted down the sky since Steele had last looked up at the window. Its glare was as strong as ever, but it struck the façades of the houses on the north side of the street at a different angle. And there was no distorting glint on the dusty panes of glass.

The Virginian ducked across the alley from the corner of the church and halted on the porch of the meeting hall. Root and Caroline Keyes were in the same postures as when he had last seen them. Their fearful eyes posed tacit questions, but Steele spoke before the injured man could voice his.

"Two mouthfuls of water a day, ma'am," he said coldly. "That because you were expecting a long wait?"

She was confused and had to shake her head to clear her mind for an answer.

"How much water did you have?" the Virginian insisted, his eyes as hard as his voice.

She swallowed hard and licked her lips, as if tasting coolness. But grimaced at the salt of the saliva which had dried around her mouth. "Four canteens, I brought, mister. I didn't figure to be here more than a day. It was for the long ride out."

"How many did you use?"

"What's this about, dude?" Root demanded.

"Shut up, feller."

Caroline swallowed again, but kept her tongue in her mouth. "One the first day. Then I started to ration myself. I got as much as two and a little more now, I guess."

"Guess again, ma'am," Steele told her, and allowed the ball of anger in his belly to deflate with a soft sigh.

"Steele!" Root called after him as the Virginian whirled and strode out into the harsh sunlight of the open street.

Grant and the Swans had crowded at the meeting hall porch to listen to the exchange. The trio were as angrily puzzled as the injured man. But they parted instinctively to allow him through. Billy made to follow him, but was jerked back into the shade and cover of the building.

"Elliott's up there, little brother," the elder Swan cautioned. And pasted an expectant grin on his thin face as he watched Steele swing around the dead man and horse, then head straight for the open gateway in the fence fronting the padre's house.

"He'll blast you, Steele!" Grant yelled.

"Reckon he's got other ideas, feller," the Virginian replied without altering his determined advance on the house.

Now, only the two women at the upper window could see the coldly grim expression carved into his lean, bristled face. And they stepped back in fear, as if unaware of what they could have done to provoke this mood in the man below.

Steele crossed the living-room of the house, empty of furniture except for an overturned three-legged stool. And went up the stairway, his footfalls heavy on the treads.

"What's the matter?" Mrs. Porter called out nervously.

Steele saw the rickety ladder sloping up into the loft and the open doorway leading to the room where the two women were waiting. Joanne Brady stepped on to the threshold, her jacket and skirt brushed clean of dust and every blemish on her face clearly visible now that the cream and powder, sweat and dirt had been scrubbed off her flesh.

She gasped and backed hurriedly into the room, seemingly forced to move by some kind of palpable power generated by the ice-cold anger emanating from the Virginian's dark eyes. She went to the old lady and

64

clung to her arm, much as she had sought the protection of Steele out on the street earlier.

"It's the man who drove the stage, isn't it?" Mrs. Porter asked, her voice shaking. But she was more afraid of Steele than of the portentous new killing.

He had halted in the doorway and was surveying the room with a bleak expression. It was spartanly furnished with a table, a narrow bed with a bedroll unfurled on it, a bureau with a cracked mirror and a group of four small religious pictures hung on a wall. There was a saddle propped against the side of the bureau. On top of the bureau was a tin basin and two canteens—lying on their sides with the stoppers out.

The two women—the older as neatly scrubbed and brushed as the younger—held their breath as they watched Steele angle across the room to the bureau.

"Oh," Joanne said as she saw the Virginian look down into the scummed water which filled the basin almost to the brim.

"We didn't . . ." Mrs. Porter started, then clutched at her throat with both hands as Steele stooped over the saddle and lifted two canteens off the horn. One made no sound when he shook it. The other sloshed with water. Not much.

When he turned to look at the women—now expressing shame-faced dismay—his own features had reformed: into the lines of a mild frown. He had long ago learned to control the temper which had been one of his worst failings as a child and young man. But it was impossible not to experience deep anger at a time such as now. But that, too, he was invariably able to swamp, with the calm reasoning that rage hampered clear thought—and was liable to trigger reckless action. It was the most futile of human emotions.

"You never did get to pray, did you?" he muttered, hooking the canteens back on the horn. "Next best thing, they say."

"What?" Joanne asked, grateful for the easy change of mood and confused by his cryptic comment.

"Cleanliness to Godliness."

"Steele?" Pat Grant yelled. "What's goin' on up there?"

"John give you the hots for the fat bitch?" Billy Swan yelled, and laughed harshly.

"Shuddup, little brother," John snarled.

Joanne loosed her hold on Mrs. Porter and both women stepped apart to allow Steele to get to the window. He lifted the latch and opened it. And looked first up at the top of the bluff, checking for the source of the rifle shot and eerie laughter. But there was just the unmoving line of solid rock against the blue emptiness of the infinite sky.

"See anythin'?" Grant asked, his voice quieter and more anxious.

Steele looked down at the three, still grouped in front of the meeting hall, with their rifles held in tight grips.

"Nothing good."

"What's that supposed to mean?" the elder Swan growled.

"It's not going to rain."

"The water!" Grant blurted, recalling the subject of the Virginian's questions to Caroline Keyes.

"We didn't think!" Mrs. Porter called shrilly as she stepped up beside Steele at the window. "We were filthy dirty and we did not consider . . ."

She, in turn, was cut off in mid-sentence. It had been a long time since any of the men had taken a drink. Too much had been happening for them to pay attention to the discomforts of the glaring heat and the parched throats it produced. But now they became bitterly aware of thirst. First linking the naked girl's answers to the confession the old woman had started to make. Then staring in horror at the burst open corpse of the man beneath the horse carcass—the ghastly scene at the center of the street driving home the knowledge that their saddles with the canteens fixed to them had been hauled out of town aboard the retreating stage.

"The stupid, friggin' cows!" Al Root shrieked from inside the meeting hall. The emptiness of the big room caused his voice to echo between the marble walls, boosting the power of his pain-tortured words.

"I'll blast 'em to hell!" Billy yelled, and raced across the street, swinging up his Winchester to aim at the window.

"Please," Mrs. Porter whimpered, and stumbled backwards.

Steele remained where he was. Only his dark eyes moved in their sockets to look towards the rim of the mesa.

A rifle shot exploded.

"Dammit to hell!" Billy cursed, his shot an accidental one triggered by the excitement of anger.

The bullet cracked from the wavering rifle barrel to blast chips of stone from the front of a store next to the padre's house.

Then another shot sounded.

Steele had seen the puff of white muzzle smoke and he grunted a moment before the sound reached the town. The report hit the street in unison with the bullet, seeming to blast eardrums with the same kind of physical force as the lead digging into the dirt two feet ahead of Swan.

The youngster screamed and skidded to a halt, halfway across the street.

The Virginian had the Colt Hartford raised, aimed and cocked by then, and his shot matched the appearance of a second puff of muzzle smoke at the top of the mesa. He saw chips of rock fly away against the blue sky as he heard the sharpshooter's rifle for a second time.

This bullet was closer to the youngster, as he whirled to race back for the cover of the meeting hall. Then a third bullet cracked past his head with only a few inches to spare as he screamed his fear of the second.

Steele had cocked the revolving rifle to try again, but stayed his gloved finger on the trigger. For, after a glimpse of a barrel in the vee-shaped cleft of a rock, nothing moved.

"You friggin' missed him, dude!" John Swan accused as his brother collapsed against the porch of the meeting hall, drawing in deep breaths of air.

"Nobody's perfect," the Virginian muttered, so that only he and the two women in the room could hear his words.

"You men down there!"

Steele had started to lower the rifle from his shoulder. Instinctively, as the eerie voice boomed out from the top of the mesa, he raised it again. But there was nothing to aim at except rock and sky.

"Root! Grant! The Swan brothers!"

"It's Elliott, the bastard!" John Swan snarled.

"Steele?" Grant called.

"Nothing," the Virginian answered, moving the rifle stock away from his shoulder and then canting the barrel to it.

"You men listen and listen good! It's your old buddy Hayes talkin' to you!" There was movement in the shaded porch of the meeting hall and Grant and the

68

Swans swung towards it, fear causing them to level their rifles.

"That poor girl!" Mrs. Porter gasped as she and Joanne came to flank Steele at the window. "The monsters!"

Joanne, concerned only with her own misery, looked down and across the street without even a mild grimace.

Caroline Keyes and Al Root had advanced to the edge of the shade, and the man undraped his arm from around the woman's shoulders to sink down to the ground. Sweat beaded his face and torso and fresh blood from the bullet wound blossomed a wider stain on the bandage around his belly. Caroline leaned gratefully against the side of the porch, exhausted from the effort of supporting the wounded man. He had allowed her to fasten the mutilated gown around her waist to form a skirt. But she was naked above her midriff, so that her punished breasts were exposed.

"Only we ain't buddies no more. Not after you double-crossed me, you sonsofbitches!"

Steele and the women at the window of the padre's house were forgotten as the men in front of the meeting hall experienced anger and confusion. And the woman stared fixedly along the street, head cocked to one side in concentration on the booming voice.

"One of you! Two, maybe! Three, or maybe all four of you! And you're gonna . . ."

"What the friggin' hell you talkin' about Hayes!" Grant yelled, crooking his rifle under an arm to cup his hands to his mouth.

". . . pay for what you done!" the man on the mesa continued without pause, his voice competing with and winning over Grant's protest. Ignoring it, perhaps, because he did not hear it.

69

"You as well, Caroline! Cause I ain't sure it wasn't you took the money! If it was you, or just one of my old buddies, the rest got a chance! By makin' the guilty party own up! You just think on that for a while!"

The silence was as weird as the booming voice as the people strained to listen to it after the final word had been directed down at Rain.

Then: "Hayes! You gone plumb outta your mind, Hayes?" Grant shrieked. "You got the money! You told us to meet you here for the share out! We ain't got nothin'! Hayes, you hearin' me!"

He kept his hands cupped around his mouth as a new silence enveloped the parched and dusty town. Then he dropped them to fasten a grip so tight to his Winchester that his knuckles showed white through the dirt ingrained into his skin.

Two puffs of white smoke appeared briefly at two points where rock intruded against the sky, about fifty feet apart. The shots sounded as one as the reports reached Rain. More divots of arid dirt were kicked up at the center of the street.

"Think of it, I said!" the familiar voice boomed.

Joanne vented a low wail and pressed clenched fists into her eyes. "Why?" she groaned between the inverted 'v' of her thick wrists. "Why should we be here? We are not a part of the evil these people are doin'. We have done no wrong."

"Who is to say why God has chosen this time and this place to punish us, my dear?" Mrs. Porter said dully. "The only certain thing is that none of us is without sin. Is that not so, young man?"

Steele shifted his bleak-eyed gaze from the younger woman to the older. "Reckon I'm not," he replied with a sigh. "But your hands look pretty clean."

# CHAPTER SEVEN

Steele understood the women's desire to freshen up after the dust and heat of the trail. Certain long established habits were difficult to lose and his appearance as he went out of the room and down the stairway was not as he liked it to be.

He had seldom, since the start of the War Between the States and the everlasting violent peace which followed it, been able to indulge his tastes for every aspect of luxurious living. But, even under the most arduous conditions, he endeavored to maintain certain standards. Thus did he purchase stylish new clothes whenever his old ones were past their prime and replacements were available. Likewise, he washed up and shaved regularly.

This was why Westerners called him "dude" and he accepted the taunt as praise. For he had been born into a closeted life of high standards and it was important for him to cling to whichever ones he could. Most he had been forced to abandon.

He had been "the dude" to the other hired guns aboard the *Queen of the River*, as the money and opportunity had been available for him to maintain appearances. For a while, at the end of the trip, he had failed to take advantage of similar opportunities. As he had ridden west, taking a different trail from the rest of the survivors, he had been in a deep slough of depression: a mood which had been alien to him since he began the drinking jag in Mexico after the death of Jim Bishop.

Nobody had died at his hand who did not deserve the ultimate punishment. But a man had been made to suffer terribly after Steele had shot his legs from under him. A man innocent of anything except a strong belief in the justice of what he intended to do. He was misguided, but then so were many others in their efforts to stop the sternwheeler reaching Twin Creeks. And many of those hired to protect the riverboat.

Of these, Steele was the most aggrieved at learning the truth about the job he was doing. But by then he was trapped, by another standard of the old code he had carried unaltered into his new life. He had accepted a man's money—and spent a great deal of it to keep up appearances—and was therefore committed to doing the job he had been hired to complete.

"Watch it, Steele!" Grant shouted as the Virginian emerged from the doorway of the padre's house and strolled casually down the walk to the gate, the Colt Hartford canted to his left shoulder.

The freckle-faced man was genuinely concerned. Billy Swan was still recovering from the terror he had experienced at the three near misses. Caroline Keyes remained locked in a private world behind the fixed stare of her eyes. Root continued to suffer great pain but watched Steele with puzzled curiosity. John Swan grinned in eager anticipation of another shot from the high mesa.

"He can pick you off like an apple in a barrel, you crazy . . ."

Mrs. Porter and Joanne Brady had been trailing Steele—staying some ten paces behind him. They gasped and whirled towards the cover of the house doorway as Grant yelled the warning. But then froze, just as Steele did, when the booming voice of the man on the mesa cut across Grant's words.

"You three others down there! This is none of your concern! And I regret that circumstances mean you must suffer! But you were not invited here! So I accept no responsibility for your fate! You can help yourselves, though! By persuadin' the guilty to confess! Only then will the sufferin' of all of you come to an end!"

This time there were three spurts of white smoke to punctuate the final word. From points along the mesa's edge different from previous shots. Again, the reports sounded as one and the bullets thudded home—two digging into the street and one burying itself in the timber of a store's sidewalk roof.

"That says it plain enough," Steele said, continuing on across the street. Behind him, the two women had begun to scamper into the house as the bullets cracked down. But they halted to listen to the Virginian. "If he plans on killing anyone, he doesn't reckon to make it as easy as a bullet."

"Hayes let you in on that before he told the whole friggin' world?" John Swan growled, his grin wiped away by a sneer.

"He did it plain enough, feller," Steele replied evenly, nodding down at the fly-covered corpse and carcass as he swung around them. "Killed the stage driver to stop him bringing help. Then dropped a galloping horse from way up there. Reckon he could have shot your kid brother as easy as . . ."

"The man's right, John," Root cut in. "Don't start seein' trouble where there ain't none. We got us enough as it is. The kind that can't be denied."

"Made worse by friggin' women!" Billy Swan snarled. Steele's contention that he had not been in danger of being shot had dissipated the final shreds of the youngster's terror. Now he was angry again as he shifted his gaze from Caroline Keyes to Mrs. Porter and Joanne.

The tortured girl was totally detached from what was happening around her, all her senses and mental resources concentrated upon whatever engaged her behind the staring green eyes.

The blemished face of Joanne Brady expressed familiar fear as she took a backward step away from the powerful rage the younger Swan directed at her.

Mrs. Porter stood her ground, a look of remorse spread over the heavily lined features. "Joanne is not to blame," she defended, her tone miserable. "We are both from the water-rich east but I am old enough to have known better. We were afraid and depressed by what had happened to us. I thought it would improve our morale to freshen ourselves up."

Pat Grant spat forcefully, arcing his spittle far out, so that when the globule found a target it sent flies buzzing angrily up from the ghastly wound of the stage driver's burst-open belly.

"It sure didn't do nothin' for *my* morale!" Root groaned.

The old lady ignored the interruptions, determined to state her apology in full—and to exonerate the plump and unattractive girl at her side. "I confess to being concerned only for myself and Joanne," she continued firmly. "And I totally failed to recall what we were told about why this town was abandoned. The water was there, and I made use of it. Not until Mr. Steele reminded me, did I realize what I had done. Now, I can do nothin' except apologize to you men. I loathe and detest all of you, but I realize I have done wrong and . . .".

"Somethin' we can do about you, old lady," John Swan rasped.

He began to swing his Winchester toward her. But his action was as slow and easy as his words, and more menacing because of it.

Steele's response was fast. A half turn from the waist, the Colt Hartford whipping down from his shoulder as his free hand came up and across, palm cupped to accept the levelled barrel. The dry click of the hammer being cocked was heard a moment before the slap of metal against buckskin.

Everyone froze, except for Billy Swan. His Winchester was still leaning against the meeting hall porch. So, as he straightened up from the wall nearby, he went for his holstered revolver.

"No!" John blurted, and made a move. Just his head—snapping it around to direct a desperate stare at Billy. He lowered his voice as the youngster's hand became a fist around the butt of the Colt but did not draw. "No, little brother."

Billy dropped his hand away from the gun and John sighed and nodded. And looked at Steele, whose lean, bronzed and stubbled face was an unmoving mask that betrayed nothing of what was going on behind the coal-black, pebble-like eyes. There was sweat on the skin, but only as much as merited by the heat of afternoon. While Swan was beaded with the salty wetness of fear. "How much they figure their nice, fresh-washed hides are worth, dude?"

"No charge, feller," Steele told the skinny, gaunt-faced man who was trying to conceal his nervousness behind a sneer.

"So what you puttin' your life on the line for them for?" Billy snarled.

"Self-interest, kid. Reckon the more people down here, the better chance I've got of getting out of Rain alive."

"You almost just died," Billy insisted.

Steele shrugged his shoulders and canted the rifle to the left once again, gloved thumb easing the hammer to the rest. "Then all my troubles would have been over."

"Thank you, sir," Joanne blurted gratefully as the tension which had been clamped over the group was abruptly lifted.

Mrs. Porter seemed on the point of rebuking the girl for her gratitude, but suddenly lacked the energy, perhaps the will. The threat of death had cancelled out whatever advantages she had derived from her misuse of the precious water and she looked very old, wearily haggard and drained of strength again.

"The man's talkin' sense," Al Root rasped through gritted teeth. "Like I already said, we got troubles enough. What we gotta do is figure out a way to deal with that bastard Hayes Elliott."

"You got any ideas, Al?" Grant asked. He was his usual sullen self again, after long moments of sweating anxiety while two rifles had been aimed and Billy had been on the point of drawing his Colt.

"Just one right now, Pat," the wounded man answered, screwing his eyes tight shut as another wave of intense agony swept over him. He paused until it had subsided. "The bitch that give me the guts ache says there's a bed across the street. Be a nice idea for you guys to carry me over there."

"Sure, Al. John. Billy. Let's make life a little easier for Al."

The younger Swan moved eagerly to help the injured

man. John held back, still smarting over the gunplay, then shifting his chagrin in the direction of Root.

But Grant spoke just as the eldest Swan was about to snarl a retort. "You got any ideas, John?" he asked, quietly but pointedly.

The anger drained out of John Swan as he looked towards the dead man and horse in the center of the street. It left him with only frustration. "Sure," he muttered with a sigh, agreeing with the implication of Grant's question rather than replying to it.

The Swans' rifles were a hindrance to their handling of the solidly built Root.

"Here," Grant said, and took the Winchesters.

Root was a very tough and a very proud man. As he was raised up from the porch and carried out into the glare of direct sunlight, agony seared through him, exploding from the point where the bullet was lodged deep inside him to travel cruelly to every nerve ending in his body. But he did not cry out. Held in a sagging curve between Billy who gripped his armpits and John who grasped his ankles, only the color and set of his features betrayed the pain he was feeling and the strain of controlling a vocal response to it. He did not screw shut his eyes until he saw the crushed body beneath the dead horse—and smelt the sickly sweet stink of lifeless flesh exposed to blistering sun. For he obviously knew that, soon, he could be a corpse himself.

Pain and fear of death prevented Root from experiencing any other sensation as he was carried across to the padre's house. Grant and the Swans feared only for their lives. Out on the open street, its surface pocked by bullet holes, it was easy for them to ignore Steele's reasoning of a few minutes ago. A man who hated them and was a crack shot was stationed up on the top of the mesa, in solid cover and with a clear view of their slow progress across the street. So they constantly glanced up at the point where rock met sky, eyes squinted and eyelids blinking against the assault of dazzling light and the sweat beads of fear.

Mrs. Porter and Joanne had made to follow them, but halted when Steele did not move. They watched the scene on the street until the group had reached the safety of the padre's house. Then returned their attention to the Virginian, looks of surprise spreading over their strained faces.

"A strange gesture from a man who pretends to be so tough," Mrs. Porter said with a slight sneer.

Steele had taken off his suit jacket and was holding it out towards Caroline Keyes. The half-naked girl was still slumped against the porch of the meeting hall, staring fixedly into infinity. But she was startled out of her private world of fear as her eyes were forced to focus on the coat. She straighened up and snapped her head around to gaze at Steele. For long moments she seemed not to recognize him. Nor the other two women and the backdrop of the dusty, sun-bright street, as her big green eyes darted their gaze this way and that.

"To cover yourself," Steele told her, and shifted his gaze from her startled face to her naked breasts.

The girl looked down at herself and grimaced at the bruises and blood on her torso. She took the coat then and put it on. "Thanks, mister," she acknowledged dully as she fastened the buttons. The jacket fitted her well although it was a little large. Between the lapels it showed more of her cleavage than the dress.

"Mr. Steele pretends nothin', Mrs. Porter," Joanne corrected and there was unconcealed admiration in her eyes as she gazed at the Virginian.

"Dude, get over here!" John Swan yelled from the

78

upstairs window of the padre's house. "Al's got an idea."

"And bring the women with you!" his brother added in the same demanding tone.

The orders were ignored for a moment.

"Is that not so, sir?" Joanne asked. "A man can be both hard and kind, I think."

"Know one thing, Miss Brady," the Virginian replied as he turned away from the trio of women. "Looking at her the way she was a while back made one part of me kind of hard."

# CHAPTER EIGHT

As he crossed the street, Steele dropped into his pants pocket the seven shells he had taken from the jacket before giving it to the girl. With the four bullets in the chambers of the rifle's cylinder, it was the only ammunition he had. Somewhere out on the barren Texas plain to the south of Rain were a half dozen cartons of .44 shells to fit the Colt Hartford. Packed into a saddlebag on the roof of the stage.

Usually, he had a larger supply on hand, chinking in the capacious pockets of a stained and torn sheepskin coat. But the coat, newly purchased for his ride to Washington for the never-to-be reunion with his father, was gone now: left aboard the burning sternwheeler as the boat cartwheeled to the whim of strong currents down the Red River.

He regretted the loss of the coat—and the stickpin with the ornate head which he had taken to concealing behind a lapel—even though he realized the foolishness of such a feeling. But to a man like Steele, with so little stability in his life, such minor details became important.

Nothing would ever be so vital to him as the Colt Hartford inherited from his father—to retain possession of which he had risked his life often. And soon, perhaps, it would be all that was left of what he had owned on that Friday night of April 14 in the year of 1865.

With the exception of the coat and gloves, he had replaced his clothes as they wore out: his penchant for cleanliness and style overruling all other considerations.

The tiny two-shot Derringer had been lost first. And he could not recall the circumstances: perhaps because the small handgun had no longer been vital to him after Jim Bishop gave him the revolving rifle. Then the first knife he had carried in the boot sheath. He had a vivid memory of seeing this go—its blade buried in the body of a man as the victim toppled off a high ledge beside a railroad track.

Now the hardworn coat was gone, along with the stickpin which had often changed from an ornament to a weapon. And he felt a mild sadness.

Perhaps he had experienced such an emotion as he rode away from Twin Creeks—first astride a horse he had accepted as a final payment for the job completed and then aboard the ill-fated stage after his mount went lame. If he had, it would have been fleetingly, for his bitterness and self-anger about all else concerned with the job had been too strong.

Now, as he stooped without breaking stride to pick up the empty Winchester discarded by Pat Grant, he silently chided himself for the futility of sentimental regret. And offered his mind a material reason for nostalgic thoughts about the sheepskin coat—the shells in its pockets.

"The situation ain't good, Steele," Grant announced morosely as he stepped off the bottom rung of the ladder sloping up into the loft.

He was carrying Caroline Keyes' yellow-boy Winchester and two cartons of shells, one of them ripped open. He spoke just as the Virginian reached the landing and the three women could be heard entering the main room below.

"You been counting our blessings, feller?" Steele asked, turning in through the bedroom doorway ahead of the freckle-faced man.

Root was stretched out on his back on the bed, sweating less than before but looking no better.

Billy had dragged Caroline Keyes' saddle into a corner and was sitting on it, grimacing down at a pile of shells on the floor between his boots. All four men had contributed to the pile from the loops in their gunbelts.

The elder Swan was at the window, head moving slowly from side to side as he surveyed the top of the mesa.

"Forty-four caliber," Grant growled, holding up the cartons. "Eighteen shells."

"We got two dozen rounds between us," Billy reported, his grimace becoming more firmly set. "Most for the handguns."

"Steele?" Root asked as the woman entered the room.

The Virginian leaned the empty Winchester against the end of the bed alongside the other rifles. "Eleven," he answered.

"Everythin' helps, I guess," the injured man rasped. "You were over here at the house most times Hayes and his new buddies opened up. How many men you figure are up there?"

Steele had gone to the window to stand beside John Swan.

"Like there ain't a livin' thing up there," the tall, skinny man muttered.

"One time three shots were fired," Steele replied to Root, his back to the room as he joined Swan in raking his gaze along the line where rock met sky. "Two shots another time. And one. From different places."

"So let's figure three, Pat," Root said. "Movin' positions to maybe make us think there are more of them."

"You didn't see no men?" Grant asked Steele. He was leaning against the doorjamb, feeding sheels into the yellow-boy Winchester.

"Angle's all wrong for that, feller," the Virginian answered. "And rocks have been stacked to give more cover."

"Elliott set us up real good!" John Swan rasped.

His brother was occupied with dividing the single heap of shells into three equal shares.

"We gotta work with what we know for sure and what we can figure out from what we know," Root growled impatiently.

"Did we come here simply to hear the obvious stated?" Mrs. Porter taunted, straightening her flowered hat on her head and then folding her thin arms across her meager breasts.

"Keep your trap shut, you old biddy!" Grant hurled at her with soft vehemence. "Al ain't never steered us wrong yet."

"Until he tied us in with that bastard Hayes Elliott!" John Swan countered bitterly as he turned from the window.

"He did all right for us on that express car job!" Root argued.

"Sure he did!" the elder brother snarled. "I'm feelin' real rich."

He put a hand in both pants pockets and jerked out the linings to expose their emptiness.

"A hundred thousand dollars would never fit in those, feller," Steele pointed out evenly.

He, too, had turned from the view of inert dark rock against unmoving bright sky.

"You tryin' to say . . ." John Swan snarled, whirling towards Steele and dropping a hand to drape his holstered Colt.

"Dammit, John!" Root yelled, and was unable to stem a grunt of pain as he raised himself on to his elbows and his belly wound protested. "And you cut it out, dude! That's just what that bastard up on the mesa is anglin' for. To get us fightin' amongst ourselves."

He fell on to his back again. But spent only a moment in staring at the ceiling before he wrenched his head to the side to share a glare between the angry Swan and the impassive Steele.

"Hold on, Al," Grant said into the fetid and tense silence that accompanied Root's glowering look. "Hayes ain't up there to sun himself. He told us his reason plain enough."

As the elder Swan's threat against him diminished, Steele shifted his easy gaze over each face in the room.

Grant had had time to adjust to the thought which Steele's remark had implanted in his mind. He was therefore making a similar survey of the Virginian but with anger mixed with the curiosity as he considered the implications.

Root and the Swans were confused, then shocked, and finally as enraged as Grant. Caroline was afraid again. Not of Steele's remark because she had been aware of the true situation in Rain ever since the man on the mesa had announced his intentions. What terrified her was the Virginian's act of reminding the others—and the way the quartet all directed their rage towards her.

"No," she gasped, and took a half step backwards which pressed her hard against the wall.

She was between Mrs. Porter and Joanne Brady, who moved hurriedly to either side: to escape the menacing stares of the four men.

"All you fellers been together since the money was hid?" Steele asked, as evenly as before.

The implication of this was as disturbing as his previous comment. And the pressure was taken off the girl as the men traded suspicious looks.

"I said to cut it out, dude!" Root snarled. He tried to fist a hand around his holstered gun. But every move he made was causing him cruel agony now and he came nowhere near to drawing.

"The man's right again, Al," Grant pointed out softly, and the sounds as he pumped the lever action of the yellow-boy were heavier with menace than any word or look would have been.

They captured the attention of everyone in the fetid room.

"Would I have come to this place to get Hayes if I'd got the money?" Caroline pleaded.

And was ignored.

"Three months ago this comin' Friday," Grant said, his tone still soft and even. He paid no attention to anybody except Root and the Swans, raking his gaze back and forth over their sweating, thickly bristled faces. "The law wouldn't give up on us as a bunch. So Hayes said we oughta split up. Throw them off that way. And that's what we done. Lit off in every direction."

"With Elliott takin' the money!" John Swan cut in.

Grant nodded. "But who's to say one of us didn't back track and take off on Hayes' trail?"

"That's crazy thinkin', Pat," Root argued, flat on his back and staring up at the ceiling again. "We all met up again in Dodge two weeks later."

"And been ridin' together ever since," Billy added.

"Sure," his brother put in. "If any one of us had the money, it sure didn't show. We ain't hardly had two dimes to rub together while we waited to hear from Elliott."

The logic of their argument was getting to Grant. And his resolve began to weaken into confusion. His mind clutched at an idea and he nodded as he held on to it.

"Hell, that figures. And we all come here runnin' when Hayes sent the telegraph."

"Which only shows that one of you is real smart!" Caroline blurted as she became the object of angry suspicion again. "And Hayes didn't count on that. He must've figured the one who took the money wouldn't show up. And there wouldn't have been none of this what's happenin'. He'd have known it was the one that was missin' took the money."

Mixed anger and confusion filled the malodorous room again, seeming to build the heat and strengthen the stinks.

"Hell, we're . . ." Root began.

And was cut off by the sounds of a rifle shot and the thud of a bullet impacting against the front of the padre's house.

Steele and John Swan whirled towards the window behind them as Billy and Grant sprang across the room to join them. But no eyes focussed on the mesa top soon enough to spot the muzzle smoke before it was dissipated.

"Mighty quiet down there!" the voice boomed and again it was impossible to pinpoint its source. "So I figure you're doin' like I told you and thinkin' on what I said!"

"Bastard!" John Swan hissed.

"Shut it!" Root growled from the bed.

"Take your time, old buddies!" the taunting voice continued. "We got food and water up here to last us a month! But I figure you ain't so well supplied. All of what you had was on the stage. So all you got is what Caroline brought in. Means you can't take too long, looks like. Couple of days? Week at the most! Then you'll all be dead as Flint and Sullivan. On account of one double-crossin' sonofabitch!"

He marked the completion of his latest message with another rifle shot. The puff of smoke showed at the top of the mesa overlooking the western end of Rain. Even before the bullet thudded bloodlessly into the unfeeling rump of the long dead horse, Grant had exploded a bullet of his own. He had barged past John Swan to extend the Winchester through the window and did not listen to the protests. He fired again. A third time. Then a fourth.

His first two shots went high and wide. The second two were low and wide.

By then John Swan had fisted a hand around the rifle barrel and jerked it downwards. Grant's snarl was still ugly as he snapped his head around to glare at the elder Swan.

". . . a friggin' waste of good lead!" Swan yelled when his voice was heard after the cracks of the exploding Winchester.

Grant looked again out of the window and up at the mass of the mesa. And he sagged as emotion drained out of him under the pressure of realization that Swan was talking sense.

Root had forced himself up on to his elbows again. Now he collapsed with a groan.

"Look," he rasped weakly, and paused to suck in hot air. His voice strengthened. "There's some sense bein' talked here. But what the frig does the stinkin' money

88

matter now? We're worse off than that bastard up there thinks we are. First we gotta get out from under. Then we can . . ."

The pain and the strain were too much for him. He raised his arms and flailed them above his chest, as if seeking some kind of physical support in the hot air to which he could grip and draw strength. But there was nothing there and he dropped his arms and closed his eyes with a sigh.

"He's dead!" Joanne blurted, and covered her fleshy and blemished face with her hands.

"Not yet," Steele corrected as the sigh ended and Root's naked chest began to rise and fall shallowly.

"Pretty soon," Billy murmured with a faint hint of regret in his voice. "And if he took the money and dies without . . ."

"Forget the money!" Mrs. Porter interrupted shrilly. And was frightened into lowering her tone as Grant and the Swans glared at her. "It's easy to see why he was your leader. Because he can forget unimportant issues to concentrate on the main one. Did we not come up here to listen to his plan for gettin' us away from this awful place?"

"No one invited you, lady!" Billy snarled.

"Shut it, Billy!" Grant ordered with a sheepish look down at the Winchester in his hands before he glanced briefly at the Virginian. "Al ain't the only smart guy in the world. Steele talked sense a while back when he said the more people we got down here the better chance we got."

"If we had friggin' Lake Erie on the back friggin' lot!" John Swan muttered.

Grant ignored him and looked morosely at the unconscious man on the bed as he spoke. "Al's idea was this. Mesa's about a mile long, right? And it ain't no army Hayes has got up there with him. And he's made it plain he doesn't wanna kill any of us. Not before he knows where the damn money is."

"Hey, that's right," Mrs. Porter exclaimed.

Even Joanne was able to raise something close to a smile of relief as the threat of death by a bullet appeared to be lifted.

"So here's what Al had in mind to do, Steele," Grant continued, no longer so confident as he directed his gaze towards the Virginian. "Two of us head out for the east end of the mesa and two go to the western end."

"Goodness, you'll be clear targets," Joanne said breathlessly. "Even if you wait until dark, the moon . . ."

"Quiet, fatso," Billy growled. "Like Al worked out, them bastards up there need info on the money before they kill us."

"Steele worked that out," Grant corrected, holding his level gaze on the Virginian's unexpressive face. "What d'you figure, Steele? If there are only three of them up there the plan's gotta bring two to one end and one to the other. Good odds . . ."

Steele was no longer listening to Grant's voice. But, even though his mind was on another time and another place, he was aware that the three men and three women were all looking expectantly at him. Behind the expectancy, there was something else—a quiet resignation to the fact that the plan would have to have the Virginian's approval if it was to be put into operation. Not only because his gun was needed to complete the quartet; in addition, Grant and the Swans missed the leadership of the unconscious Root and needed a replacement. For their part, the women sensed the trio's doubt of their own ability and were thus left with Steele as the only man in whom to place their trust.

His mind, as Grant continued to sell the plan, was concerned with a memory of a Mississippi community called Bradstock Landing. There had been two men there who needed to be taken alive. A reckless reaction to danger had killed one of the men. Steele had been icily calm in dealing with the second, aiming a long range shot at a fast moving target, and seeing him pitch to the ground as the bullet from the Colt Hartford shattered a kneecap.

"I'm thirsty enough to give it a try," he replied as he became conscious of the silence and realized an answer was expected of him.

"You think we oughta wait until night, dude?" John Swan asked gruffly, resentful of the need to seek advice from a man he detested.

"Full moon last night," Steele reminded. "And I don't reckon we'll get any cloud cover tonight."

"So we go now?" Billy asked, glancing nervously about the room, suddenly deeply aware of the security it offered.

"No time like the present," Steele said, then added: "For a man who's thirsty to take a drink."

The elder Swan and Pat Grant had become infected with the same brand of fear as Billy. It dried all their throats. And Steele's mention of thirst added to the arid tightness. Caroline Keyes and Joanne Brady were no longer afraid. But Steele had reminded them of the lack of water and they licked their dry lips with tongues which felt swollen.

"But won't they . . . ?" Mrs. Porter began.

The Swans and Grant were prepared to listen to her objection. For talk meant they could remain in the squalid, oven-hot, stinking room for a few more minutes.

"Men go to war while women stay home and worry,

ma'am," Steele cut in, trapping her anxious gaze in a hard-eyed stare that demanded silence. "And men fight better with just the one thing in mind. Winning."

"Let's go, Steele!" Grant snapped. "You and me to the east. John and Billy to the west."

He was content with Caroline Keyes' yellow-boy Winchester. The Swans claimed their own rifles and gathered up handfuls of shells from the floor to push through the loading gates of their weapons. Grant gazed up at the mesa from the window. Caroline was peering into infinity again, apparently not seeing the dying Al Root who was in direct line of her vision. Joanne stared at the basin of scummed water, the sight serving to sharpen her thirst.

So that only Steele saw the old lady's nod of understanding as she finally read the tacit message in his dark, cold eyes.

"I wish you well, young man," she said, softly and sincerely.

"Hey, dude!" John Swan called as he completed loading the Winchester and began to slot shells into his gunbelt. He tried for a light-hearted tone, but there was a crack in it. And his attempt at a sneering smile made him appear to be on the verge of throwing up. "You sure got winnin' ways with women. You wanna let us in on your secret?"

"No secret, feller," Steele answered, striding across the room towards the open door. "Just take them as they come."

The elder Swan attempted a laugh now. It had a hollow sound of pretence. "I just take 'em, dude! Don't give a shit whether they come or not!"

# CHAPTER NINE

As Steele moved slowly along the eastern stretch of Rain's only street, he was conscious of being watched by several pairs of eyes. There was constant vigilance from the top of the mesa and the upstairs window of the padre's house. And he was also the object of fleeting glances from Pat Grant who walked beside him and the Swan brothers who were heading out of town in the opposite direction.

But there was a threat from only one source and it was there that he directed his full attention. Cracking his eyes to the narrowest of slits to rake their intent gaze from one spot on the mesa's top to the other, he marked the points of effective rifle range to where he and Grant were at the particular moment.

He held the Colt Hartford slantwise across the front of his body, the muzzle moving back and forth on the same track as his eyes, one gloved hand fisted around the barrel and the other at the frame. His thumb had cocked the hammer as he came out of the padre's house and his index finger had taken first pressure against the trigger.

The other three men moving along the exposed street carried their rifles in the same attitude. They interrupted their survey of the mesa's skyline only to check that the Virginian was continuing to act in the same manner.

Reluctant to take a hand off his Winchester, Grant tossed his head to fling sweat beads off his forehead and eyelids.

"I guess you figure the Swans and me are pretty dumb, uh, Steele?" the freckle-faced man asked, his voice a rasping whispered.

"Never think about other folks' problems unless I'm paid to, feller," came the even-voiced response.

"It wasn't no problem while Al was frontin' us," Grant went on, seeming to draw some comfort from the sound of his own sullen-toned voice. "He never did steer us wrong until he tied in with Hayes Elliott. And there weren't no way to tell it was gonna be a double-cross. Job went like a dream until the law wouldn't give up on us. Then it was the smartest thing to do. Split up."

"No time to split up the take, feller?" Steele posed.

He maintained his watch on the craggy line where rock and sky met, just blinking now and then to shake blurring sweat from his eyelids and to combat the strain of the dazzling stare from infinite blueness.

"Yeah, I guess there was," Grant said bitterly. "But there just weren't no reason not to trust Hayes. He seemed like a straight guy. And Al said he was all right."

"And you trust Root."

Steele began to sweat more now, as he and Grant moved out from between the two houses at the end of the street and on to the open trail. There was a bad smell from the house on the left. A familiar stink. The odor of decomposing flesh.

Grant's nostrils wrinkled and he supplied: "The Keyes woman's horse. She told us. When she run outta food, she butchered it. Meat turned rotten after two days."

"I said do you trust Root, feller?" Steele reminded.

Paradoxically, a heat that felt more powerful than that of the sun and which caused the sweat to erupt on every pore of his body, was generated by an ice cold ball of fear compacted at the pit of his stomach. For he knew he was in greater danger of imminent death than any of the other men who were leaving the cover of the town behind them. For those on the top of the mesa could afford to blast him into the Texas ground as an example which would cost them nothing.

"I heard you!" Grant snarled. "Yeah, I trust Al. It's them two Swans I don't . . ."

A tell-tale puff of white smoke smudged the line between dark rock and glaring sky. At a midway point on the mesa, directly opposite the meeting hall on one side of the street and the padre's house on the other.

Steele and Grant both swung into a half turn and dropped into a half-crouch, rifle stocks thudding against their shoulders.

The reports were a fraction of a second apart. The crack of the gunshot from the mesa filled the gap. John Swan's scream came immediately afterwards.

Then: "You sonofabitch, Elliott!" Billy shrieked, swinging his rifle to blast a wild shot high into the air.

John was on the ground now, raising a cloud of dust as he writhed there, his rifle discarded so that he could clutch at a blood-spurting ankle with both hands.

Steele and Grant lunged forward, sprinting for the cover of the first house under the mesa.

"Save it!" the Virginian snarled as Grant loosed off a shot on the run, his bullet cracking as high and wide as Billy Swan's.

Three more patches of muzzle smoke showed, closely

followed by two more. Then one. All at different points along a thirty-foot stretch of the mesa's center length.

Billy Swan cursed louder than his brother's shrieks of agony as three bullets dug up divots of trail close by him. A moment later, two bullets pocked the east trail several feet beyond where Steele and Grant had been caught in the open. The final shot ripped an obscenity from Grant's snarling lips as the bullet ploughed a shallow furrow across the side of his thigh.

With blood blosssoming into a large stain from the jagged rent in his pants, the freckle-faced man sank on to his haunches with his back against the front of the house.

Steele remained upright, enjoying a sense of well-being as the fear flowed out of him. The man on the mesa had chosen to ignore the stranger and punish only those he had intended to come to Rain. It had been a fifty-fifty chance and the luck by which he set little store continued to hold for Steele.

"Billy, you asshole!" Grant yelled. "Get yourselves off the damn trail!"

John was sitting up, back arched and arms stretched to wrap his hands around his shattered right ankle. His younger brother was still raking the muzzle of his rifle back and forth along the mesa top. But nothing could be seen to move up there. The silence which Grant had broken with his shrill warning continued as soldily and oppressively as before.

Steele listened to it for stretched seconds, then stepped away from the wall of the house.

"What the frig?" Grant snarled.

"He's through with us for a while," the Virginian replied evenly as he crossed the dusty garden and the rotted wood of the collapsed picket fence snapped dryly under his boots.

It was as if the man above the town had heard the soft-spoken comment and felt it should be amplified.

"You people down there!" the booming voice intoned. "You been thinkin', but you been thinkin' on the wrong lines. Ain't no way you can get up here to us. And only one way you can get outta Rain alive. All but the guilty party, that is. That'll be when you send him up to me!" There was a short pause. "Or her. So best you get back to the house and think on that!"

Everyone in the town waited for the crack of a rifle to announce the end of the speech. But there was no sound to break the silence which was more menacing than a fusillade of gunfire would have been.

Steele started back along the street, ejecting the empty shell case from the Colt Hartford and fitting a fresh bullet into the smoke-smelling chamber.

Grant followed him at a limping run to catch up. At the western edge of town, Billy Swan picked up his brother's rifle and then accepted John's arm around his shoulder to support him on the way back.

The Virginian continued to look up at the mesa, but his rifle was canted easily to his left shoulder now. And there was a thoughtful frown on his face. But Grant's mind was busy with other things and he failed to take note of Steele's expression.

"If Hayes ain't doin' this for some kinda crazy reason, it was one of the Swans took the money," he rasped. "Or maybe the both of 'em. If it was just the one, it'd be John."

Steele nodded, but not in response to the other man's reasoning. Certain features on the rock face of the bluff had given him enough points of reference to reach a decision about the rifle fire which had been poured down on Rain.

"Either of them be smart enough to come here, feller? If they had . . ."

"Look!" Grant cut in. "Ain't none of us got more than a lick of sense between us. Not countin' Al, that is. I mean me and the Swans and Sullivan and Flint. But we know what we're entitled to. And we'd go to hell and back if that's what it took to get our entitlement. We know that about each other, make no mistake. So the man that took that money knows he won't never get to spend it unless the rest of us are dead."

"Two are, feller," Steele reminded as he and the limping Grant reached the gate in the fence fronting the padre's house. "And one almost."

"Wrong, young man," Mrs. Porter announced from the upstairs window. "Mr. Root has passed from our midst."

Grant snapped up his head to look at the lone woman at the window. Then vented a grunt of dismay and cursed at the injured leg which slowed his progress up the walk and into the house.

"What's Pat's hurry?" Billy Swan asked, breathless from the effort of half-carrying his wounded brother.

Steele was looking up at the mesa top again.

"Mr. Root has gone," the old lady answered for him.

"Gone?" Billy snarled, lunging forward so that John crumpled hard to the ground with a shrill scream of fresh agony. "Gone where?"

"To friggin' hell, you crazy bastard!" John shrieked, struggling to shift the weight of his body off his shattered ankle. "That's certain," he said less stridently as his pain subsided and Billy skidded to a halt halfway up the walk. " 'Cause it's for sure ain't none of us bound for heaven."

The younger brother seemed close to tears as he snapped his head around, looking from John, to Steele and then to Mrs. Porter. "What we gonna do now?" he wailed.

"You can pray that God will have mercy on his soul," the gray-haired, crinkle-faced woman offered.

Billy snorted.

John spat at a patch of his blood soaking into the dust of the street. "Looks like the dude's already takin' care of that," he growled, nodding towards Steele who still had his head tilted back, eyes narrowed to peer upwards.

"I doubt if any of you know how to pray," Mrs. Porter countered with her lips set thin in a sneer of disgust.

"I know it's said He helps those who help themselves, ma'am," Steele replied, ending his survey.

"Well I can't help myself get to my friggin' feet!" John Swan snarled as his younger brother disappeared into the house.

John shifted his pained and angry gaze from the empty doorway to the face of the Virginian—which was without expression as he drawled a reply: "Know how you feel, feller. I can't stand you, either."

# CHAPTER TEN

The afternoon grew older but as the sun slid down the western dome of the sky the heat did not diminish. And the tension of unspoken hatred built up.

The body of Al Root was over at the church, dragged there unceremoniously by Billy Swan who had laid the corpse beside those of Sullivan and Flint in front of the altar.

John Swan was on the bed, his wound not bound. The flies had ceased to bother him after a crusting of black blood had formed over the entry and exit holes of the damaging bullet. Numbness deadened the pain and his hate was directed at Steele, who had left him out on the street, exposed to the sun and a killing shot, until an obscene tirade had summoned his brother to bring him inside.

Billy had reclaimed his seat on the saddle in the corner. Initially, just as John suffered pain, Billy had endured grief. Perhaps simply for the death of Root, more probably because he considered that the man's passing lowered the chances of his own survival. Then, after he recognized the futility of this, he began to work up a hate: his dully gleaming eyes constantly straying their gaze towards Pat Grant.

The wound in the flesh of the freckle-faced man was only superficial. It brought a grimace of pain to his features whenever he placed weight on his right leg, but caused him no discomfort as he sat on the ledge of the window, angling his hatred up towards the man who was tormenting them all from the safety of the mesa's top.

Mrs. Porter hated Steele. She and Joanne Brady sat on the floor to one side of the open doorway. At first, she had caught the Virginian's attention often, asking a question with her own eyes but receiving no response from his. Then, gradually, her disgust of him deepened to something more powerful as she realized he had no intention of building on the rapport which had seemed to exist between them before the latest shootings.

Joanne and Caroline Keyes—the latter sitting on her haunches in the corner diagonally across from Billy Swan—were unaware of the mounting tensions within the hot and malodorous confines of the room. For both had withdrawn into the private realms of their own individual fears. The fleshy girl kept her eyes tightly closed. The tortured one stared sightlessly up at the angle where a wall met the ceiling.

Steele was on his haunches with his back against the bureau, his hat brim pushed forward down his forehead and his gloved hands loosely gripping the Colt Hartford resting across his thighs. He seemed to be asleep, but his eyes were open in the deep shadow of the hat brim, which was not down low enough to block off his view of every face except that of Pat Grant.

There had been a great deal of angry talk at first, after the latest corpse had been taken into the church and the survivors were all gathered in the room again. With the two women watching and listening fearfully and Steele responding in an even tone when the taunts and abuse were linked with his name.

It was the Virginian who ended the barrage of words when he said: "Don't reckon you people are going to talk that feller down off the mesa."

"You got an idea, Steele?" Grant had asked eagerly.

"Maybe."

"What?" From Billy Swan.

"Needs night, kid."

"But you can tell us now," John pointed out.

"Have patience, feller. Test whether the opposition has got any."

There could have been another explosion of angry words then. But the interlude of relative quiet in the room had brought a soothing effect. The Swans, Grant and Mrs. Porter were suddenly aware that their rage had subsided and they had no inclination to build the fires of strong feelings again. Perhaps they did not have the energy after their reserves had been drained by the pain, fear, tension and anger of the attempted escape and its aftermath of bitter frustration.

But the lull could not last and, as the hot minutes slid wearily into the past, Steele waited for the mixed emotions of his fellow-prisoners to crystallize into volatile hatred and watched for the first sign of a dangerous blow-up.

Billy Swan shifted his position slightly on the saddle, and said: "It's gotta be you, Grant."

Steele moved a hand, but only to tip up the brim of his hat so that he could see the entire room. He dropped the hand back to the rifle, thumb against the hammer.

Everyone looked at the youngster and saw that his thin face continued to wear the strained frown which his features had formed while he was reaching the conclusion.

"Was thinkin' the same about you and your big brother, Billy," Grant replied.

The younger Swan's tone had been soft but venomous. The older man's voice was flat and as he turned from the window, leaning just a hip on the ledge, Steele saw from his freckled profile that Grant was taut with anger on a tight leash.

Billy and John both opened their mouths as their eyes told of uncontained rage. But Pat Grant spoke first, and his unemotional tone held the brothers in check.

"Wasn't Flint or Sullivan. They didn't have a backbone worth a bent nickel between them. If it'd been either one he'd have yelled it loud and clear before Hayes started to hack off his hands."

"Ain't got no argument with that," John Swan allowed huskily.

Grant ignored him: concentrating his cold-eyed stare on Billy. "And Al . . . well, he just wouldn't have done nothin' like that. He was a straight guy all the way down the line."

This time the elder Swan merely nodded.

Grant inclined his head to one side to indicate Caroline Keyes, who was once more fearfully aware of her surroundings and those who peopled them. "I go along with the story Hayes' woman told us. She didn't know none of us nor what we're like. If she took the money she'd have just lit out. Killed Hayes maybe, but just like she didn't know us, we didn't know what she looked like."

Caroline blinked once and the fear was abruptly gone from her green eyes. And it was as if her terror had slid out of her, slithered across the dusty floor and insinuated itself into the mind of John Swan. For the icy calmness of Pat Grant's voice and attitude had got to the elder brother. Grant spoke with conviction and

Swan realized he was agreeing with everything that was said.

"She figured Al was Hayes Elliott!" he blurted out, but immediately lost the thread of his argument.

"Because he ditched her for another woman and . . ."

"And took the money!" John cut in with a crooked-toothed smile of triumph that his mind had found a substantial thought to cling to. "That's it, Pat! Elliott has had it all the time. He just wants to kill us all so we won't be around to go after him while he's blowin' it!"

Grant shook his head. "Can't be that way. Steele said it and Hayes proved it. He could've gunned us down easy, but he didn't."

John Swan swallowed hard, his hope dashed as the ice of cold fear crushed his mind again.

"Like I said," Grant went on. "I'm buyin' his woman's story. But I figure Hayes made his Mexico plans before he went to get the money from where he stashed it. When he got there, it was gone."

"But she said he planned to take the whole friggin' bundle!" John tried again. But he did not build his hopes this time. The turmoil in his mind did not allow him to project his objections and he seemed to know that Grant would have an undeniable counter to everything he said.

"Maybe he did," the freckle-faced man allowed flatly. "But that don't matter a shit now. It sure as hell does matter that he ain't got one cent of the friggin' bundle."

He spat from the side of his mouth without turning his head. And the globule of saliva arced out through the window to spatter on the sun-heated walk below. "And I sure as hell ain't got it."

He drew his Colt. He was not fast, but he had all the advantages. John Swan was deep in a slough of conflicting emotions and thoughts as his mind raced to assimilate all that Grant had said and to reach a conclusion. And his younger brother looked at him at the wrong moment.

Up until a second before Grant went for the gun, Billy had been unmoved by the talk. He had spent a long time building up his conviction that Grant pulled the double-cross, and steadfastly refused to have his belief shaken. Until he allowed his gaze to touch his brother's face. He had only intended for it to be a brief glance: to check that John was prepared to back him. But he saw the look in his brother's eyes, which happened to be directing their doubt towards him.

That was when Grant drew, as Billy's head was turned and the expression on the youngster's face altered from hatred to desperation.

"John!" Billy wailed. "He's tryin' to . . ."

The elder Swan was suddenly aware of the danger. And that he had given Grant the opportunity to get the drop on his brother.

"No, little . . ." he screamed across the wailed plea.

Billy dropped a hand to his gun and started to power up from the saddle. His thin face, pulled into an expression of utter wretchedness, was still turned towards John, while his Colt cleared the holster to swing up at Grant.

Joanne Brady screamed and covered her eyes.

Mrs. Porter's sole reaction was to set her lips into a tight, thin line.

Caroline Keyes expressed something close to a smile, but Steele could not be sure of this as he shifted his unexpressive gaze from her to Grant.

The freckle-faced man had lost his composure. He seemed to be suffering the same degree of mental torture as Billy Swan. For he had not intended that his response to the youngster's opening comment should reach this stage. And he had no way of knowing whether it would be Billy's head or his gun hand which would turn. To wait for the matter to be settled could cost him his life.

He squeezed the trigger. The big Colt bucked in his fist. Billy was knocked back down on to the saddle by the impact of the bullet. His head snapped around and his eyes widened in surprise as a spout of bright crimson fountained from his left upper arm.

Grant expressed surprise of his own.

"Billy, I don't . . ."

The youngster's gun hand had sagged when he fell on to the saddle. But it swung up again, his thumb cocking the hammer as the surprise left his face and hatred cut deep lines in the sweat-run flesh again.

Grant had cocked his own Colt as a reflex action after blasting the first bullet from a chamber. He knew words would not stop Billy. So he fired a second time and cursed as the bucking .45 placed the bullet into the youngster's right hip. Again the impact of a heavy caliber bullet smashing into his flesh spoiled Billy's aim.

"You sonofabitchin' bastard!" the twice-wounded Swan rasped, half sprawled across the saddle now as he struggled to get the Colt back on target.

John Swan went for his gun.

Steele unfisted his right hand from around the barrel of the Colt Hartford. And delved it into the split seam on the outside of his right pants leg.

Grant's gun exploded a third time.

The bullet tunneled into Billy's lower face, smashing

through his bristled chin, shattering crooked teeth and exiting at the nape of his neck after holing the back of his throat. His dying sound was a scream which began shrill and then was swamped by the bloody spray from his gaping mouth.

Grant wasted precious time as he stared in horror at the corpse, twitching to the dictates of a punished nervous system. But he did not pay the price of his mistake.

For Steele had drawn the knife from his boot sheath and powered half erect to give added impetus to his underarm throw.

The knife spun, blade over handle, through hot air in which acrid gunsmoke drifted.

John Swan was supporting himself on his left elbow and his right arm was extended to its full reach: the gun clenched in the fist was aimed directly at the unmoving form of Grant.

The Colt cracked, but the bullet thudded harmlessly into the window ledge as Swan screamed. For the trigger had been squeezed by an involuntary movement of a nerve, as the point of the knife dug into the wrist of the gun hand. The force of the throw slammed the whole length of Swan's arm against the wall, but the knife still had momentum and its blade sank deeper into flesh, missing bone. And the point burst out of the other side and finally came to a halt—buried in the adobe which coated the walls of the rooms.

"Let me loose!" Swan shrieked after his scream had been curtailed by a choking cough. His fingers splayed open and the gun dropped to the bed.

"I didn't mean to kill Billy," Grant said dully, raking his pleading gaze over every face in the room after the second act of violence had wrenched him out of his horrified stare at the corpse.

"Reckon not, feller," the Virginian said as he crossed the room, pressed the stockplate of his rifle against Swan's forearm, grasped the knife and wrenched it from the flesh. Against the shrillness of the agonized man's scream, he muttered: "Things just got out of hand."

# CHAPTER ELEVEN

A rifle shot exploded from outside the room, high on the mesa which towered above Rain in back of the south side of the street.

"What's goin' on down there? Why all the shootin'?"

The bullet had shattered glass in a window below. Pat Grant instinctively stepped away from the bedroom window and flattened himself against the wall beside it.

"Don't show yourself, feller," Steele rasped. "Everybody stay clear of the window."

"You ain't so sure of him now, dude?" Grant snarled.

"Reckon he's not so sure of himself," the Virginian drawled evenly.

More rifle fire. Six shots in quick succession from a single gun triggered by an angry man venting his feelings on inanimate objects. The roof of the church. A store window. The dusty street. Then a return to self-control which enabled him to place a trio of shots into the padre's house through the open doorway.

"You ain't thinkin' right! Like before! I want that money!" The booming effect of the voice masked its tone. But the man was talking faster than before, as a further indication of his anger.

Swan sucked at the bloody wound on the inside of his wrist, droplets of crimson dripping on to his shirt from the outside. Tears of pain or grief squeezed from his eyes as he stared at the crumpled and stained corpse of his brother.

Joanne continued to hide her pimpled face behind her pudgy hands, a low moaning sound trickling from her trembling lips.

A strange sneer twisted the mouthline of Caroline Keyes as she indulged in cruel enjoyment of Swan's suffering.

After his snarling outburst, Grant had become silently quizzical, watching the impassive Virginian. His gun seemed to be forgotten in his hand until Swan growled,

"Look what you done to Billy, you bastard!"

Grant tensed then, and swung his gun towards the man on the bed. But the rigidity drained out of him when he saw that Swan was helpless. Incapacitated by two wounds and with the Winchester and Colt both out of his reach.

Mrs. Porter watched all of this with knowing eyes and lips slightly cracked open to show teeth clenched together.

There had been a brief silence from the top of the mesa. Then, "You start thinkin' right, down there! You send me up the one that took the money!"

They all waited for a shot, but none came. They listened to the silence, for a long time. Until the sun sank low enough so that the shadow of the mesa reached into the room through the open window.

Grant sighed, then showed a brutal grin. "We rattled the bastard."

"Billy's life weren't worth that, you sonofabitch!" John Swan countered.

The freckle-faced man looked balefully at the corpse, and pushed the revolver back into his holster. "It

112

weren't meant to be that way, John. I just figured to get the drop on him. Then beat the friggin' truth outta him. Or outta you!"

He tried to inject heavy menace into the final statement. But, just as had happened earlier, he found he had been drained of the energy to create stronger feeling.

Swan recognized this and experienced much the same thing. He flopped back to sprawl out full length on the bed and allowed his injured hand to rest across his stomach. The flies buzzed in to feed.

"We're beat, Pat," he said morosely as he stared dejectedly up at the ceiling. "You know, same as I do, Billy wouldn't have took that friggin' money. Not unless he cut me in on it."

"Like I said," Grant answered without force as his features re-formed into their customary sullen set, "or outta you."

Swan ignored the repeated accusation for a while. "Billy mighta taken it into his head to double back and trail Elliott. And he mighta stole the cash. But he couldn't've kept a secret like that from me. You know that." He raised his head to stare across the room at Grant. "And if Billy was still alive, I'd swear on my little brother's life I didn't get that express car money, Pat."

"You're all stupid!" Joanne Brady hurled out from under her hands. Then dropped her arms to expose her blemished face. "You're killin' each other off for nothin'! It's been said. The money doesn't matter. We've got to get out of this horrible place. When you do that, then you stupid people can . . ."

She had pushed herself up from the floor. And, as she rose, so did the note of hysteria in her voice. Her

113

complexion became crimson and her eyes gleamed. She clenched and unclenched her fists and began to shake her head violently from side to side.

It was the crack of Mrs. Porter's hand against a glowing cheek which halted the tirade.

The girl stared at the old lady and froze, hands half unfolded so that her fingers were like talons. Just for part of a second, it looked as if she might bring up her arms and claw at Mrs. Porter. But then tears squeezed from her eyes, a sob escaped her throat and she flung herself at the woman, embracing her like a frightened child seeking the comfort of her mother.

Mrs. Porter responded to the embrace and twisted her head to look back over her shoulder. There was deep scorn in her wrinkled face.

"Has it not occurred to you that a complete stranger might have taken the filthy money?" she snapped.

"Goddamnit!" Grant barked.

"Sonofa—" Swan augmented.

Both men stared hard at each other as the implications of the old lady's comment became deeply embedded into their minds.

"It's what's been concerning me from the start," Steele said softly.

Caroline Keyes had detached herself from reality again. She stared fixedly at the corpse of Billy Swan and appeared to be totally oblivious to what was happening around her.

But everyone else snapped their attention toward the Virginian. Even Joanne raised her tear-moist face from the old woman's thin shoulder to look at him. And there was a mixture of incredulity and horror on every face.

"Then why the friggin' hell didn't you say somethin', you asshole?" Grant demanded.

"Because nobody paid him!" Mrs. Porter snarled, backing away from the clinging girl.

"Crap!" Swan countered. "He was told he was in for a share."

"The bastard's parlayin' it into a bigger share every time one of us gets friggin' dead!" Grant snapped.

He seemed poised to draw his Colt again. But he read what was behind the Virginian's apparent nonchalance. Steele had wiped the blood from the knife on a bedroll blanket and replaced the weapon in its sheath. Then he had moved to the doorway, where he now stood, the Colt Hartford sloped casually to his left shoulder. But his gloved hand was on the frame with his thumb on the hammer. And there was grim intent in the impassive set of his features, a certain tautness in the way the skin stretched over his bristle jaw and the look in his dark eyes under the hat brim.

"Share of what, feller?" he asked.

"The friggin' money!" Grant hurled back.

"What money?"

Grant blinked.

Swan gtunted, then rasped: "He's right."

"You cold-blooded monster!" Mrs. Porter accused, shock making her breathless. "You've been waitin' around here like some ugly buzzard. Waitin' . . . waitin' . . . yes, waitin' for the richest tastin' corpse!"

Joanne Brady gasped when she saw that Steele remained icily calm in face of the old lady's abuse. Then shook her head in disbelief.

"No!" She pointed to Grant. "Mr. Steele saved his life," she defended.

"For his own evil ends!" Mrs. Porter came back, continuing to pour scorn over Steele with her eyes.

"I sure didn't owe him anything, ma'am," the Virginian allowed.

"You figure he took the money, dude?" Swan asked, suddenly excited and eager.

"You ain't in the clear with him, asshole!" Grant warned. "He coulda put that sneaky knife in your heart!"

Swan was shocked, then abruptly dejected. "Yeah," he growled.

Joanne Brady turned and moved with slow resolution towards the doorway where Steele stood. Her face was now very pale, emphasizing the angry pimples and the mark where Mrs. Porter had slapped her. As she gazed into Steele's face she expressed a greater degree of contempt for him than Mrs. Porter was showing.

"I'd like you to step aside and let me pass, please," she demanded, her voice crisp and distinct.

"Where are you goin', dear?" the old lady asked anxiously as the Virginian touched the brim of his hat with his free hand and did as requested.

The girl halted on the threshold of the room and looked back over her shoulder. "I'm tired and hungry and thirsty. I'm also afraid and disgusted. And I'm goin' to meet my fiancé in Fort Worth."

"You'll never make it," Steele warned evenly.

"Those men up there will not shoot me," the girl maintained. "I have nothin' they want, so they have no interest in me."

"There's only miles and miles of desert country out there, Joanne!" Mrs. Porter said quickly. "And it's nearly nightfall. If you don't die from exposure, the sun will . . ."

"So be it," came the calm response. "If I am to die, I would rather it be in the clean, open air. Away from the filth and the stink of this horrible town. You are welcome to come with me, Mrs. Porter."

The old lady was disconcerted, for the first time in

many hours. She looked hurriedly about her. At the evil smelling room and its occupants. At a corpse crusted with blood. At three men she held in the utmost contempt. At one girl who had been physically tortured—apparently to the verge of madness. And at another who was proposing an insane plan.

"I know I will not get to Fort Worth, Mrs. Porter," Joanne went on. "That I will never see Lieutenant Brannigan again. But whether I am to die twenty miles from here or right outside the door of this house, it will be better than perishin' in such company as this."

The old lady looked around her again, and was persuaded. "Yes, my dear. You're quite right. We are doomed whatever happens."

"You're friggin' crazy, that's what you are!" Swan rasped. "The both of you. That sonofabitch Elliott won't take no chance on you makin' it. He'll blast you good. Just like he did the old guy who drove the stage."

This reminder of the rotting, burst-open body on the street brought Mrs. Porter up short in the doorway.

There continued to be a reversal of the former roles between the two women as the younger one smiled serenely at the abruptly frightened old one.

"You've got nothing to lose but your lives, ladies," Steele said.

"But you will not deny us the freedom to choose when we lose them, sir?" Joanne countered.

She was no longer smiling. Steele was close enough to see the fear in back of her eyes, and the fine sweat sheening her forehead. She expressed no plea, but he sensed she was crying out deep inside her for him to stop her completing what she had started.

"Everyone makes mistakes," the Virginian told her. "Up to you if you want this to be your last one."

Both women looked set to question Steele: to ask

117

him to amplify what he-had said. But Grant spoke first.

"Frig off and get yourselves killed! I'm gonna get outta this stinkin' ghost town alive, I know that. And when I do, I'm gonna be rich!"

"Money!" Mrs. Porter snapped and there was a sudden return to authority in her voice and manner. "Disgustin' greed! You will all die because of it! Come, my dear."

Joanne Brady was trembling and afraid. Steele glimpsed her fleshy face for just a moment before the older woman strode across the threshold and forced her to back out on the landing: and he saw the torment of terror which was attacking the girl. At first she had been sure of herself—convinced she was doing the right thing. But the Virginian's soft-spoken words had insinuated doubts into her mind: a mind that was delicately balanced between hysteria and rational thought.

Then she was gone, Mrs. Porter taking hold of her upper arm, turning her, and steering her along the landing and down the stairway. The old lady's booted feet rapped on timber. Joanne's bare feet padded.

"Damn crazy women!" Swan snarled, screwing his head around to stare at the empty doorway. But in back of his wild eyes there was bitter disappointment. Not because they were leaving, instead because he was denied the opportunity to make such a choice. For he was as frightened as they were.

So was Grant, as the freckle-faced man grimaced across the room at the Virginian. "You change your mind, Steele?" he demanded. "You said the more of us against Hayes and his men the better chance we got. They're women, but they could shoot guns. They could . . ."

Steele advanced on him, swinging the Colt Hartford down from his shoulder. Unhurried. Grant cursed and backed away. But the Virginian was merely seeking the vantage point of the window and his tone was calm as he said: "Get ready to give them some covering fire, feller."

"Waste friggin' shells on them?" Grant snapped. "Let 'em get blasted to hell for all I care!"

"Suit yourself," the Virginian replied, nestling the rifle's stockplate against his shoulder and elevating the barrel to take aim at the midway point along the mesa's top.

It was evening, with just the trailing arc of the sun still above the western horizon. The light it emanated was dark red at its source, but shaded into pale pink further out. The line where rock touched sky was easy to look at now. There was no need to squint against harsh glare.

As he heard the two women emerge from the house onto the walk and come to a halt, he sensed they had become aware of his presence above them and were looking up at him. And he thought briefly about innocence and guilt. The man who had tried to cut the *Queen of the River* loose from her moorings had been an innocent. But Steele could excuse himself up to a point, for there had been no way of knowing this until later.

The two women who were now offering him a final chance to protect them from almost certain death? Joanne Brady was a total innocent. And Mrs. Porter, too. Although Steele had always suspected the old lady had an ulterior motive in using the water to such a useless end. A good one.

"Come, my dear," she urged.

And their footfalls sounded the different notes of boots and bare skin against the walk.

Steele's jawline tightened as his gloved finger took

119

first pressure against the trigger of the rifle. He was one of the guilty ones, for his motives since becoming trapped in the abandoned town had never been laudable. Everything he had done had been directed towards the single aim of capitalizing on his situation. To the exclusion of all other considerations, including the protection of the innocent.

Which was nothing new, he concluded as he continued to direct his eyes towards the top of the mesa while the women went through the open gateway and turned east along the street. That had been his way ever since the beginning of the violent peace, based upon the clear-cut philosophy that freedom was the most vital quality of life after life itself.

The tell-tale puff of muzzle smoke showed up more clearly against the dark rock in the subdued light of evening.

Steele adjusted the aim of the Colt Hartford six feet to the right. The report sounded simultaneously with the thud of the bullet into the surface of the street. Joanne Brady's cry of alarm came a moment later.

"Just keep walkin', my dear!" Mrs. Porter urged, unable to keep the shrillness of her own fear out of her voice.

"He hit one of 'em, Pat?" Swan demanded from the bed, still afraid. Not for the lives of the women as such: rather of the continued presence of death in Rain.

"You women!" the voice boomed from above as Grant swung away from the wall to peer tentatively out of the window. "Where the hell do you think you're goin'?"

"Out of here, you brutal monster!" Mrs. Porter countered. But terror constricted her vocal chords and her words barely reached into the bedroom of the padre's house.

"You better not try to leave!" the man shouted down. "Hey, you men! You better get them women to turn back! Or I'll kill 'em for sure!"

The bedspring creaked as Swan moved. Bare footfalls padded across floorboards as Caroline Keyes emerged from her world of private contemplation and rose to go towards the twice-wounded man.

"They ain't stoppin', Steele," Grant reported in a rasping whisper.

"Their choice," the Virginian replied, continuing to devote his full attention towards the mesa's skyline.

"I friggin' warned you!"

The puff of white muzzle smoke.

A just discernible change in the shape of the mesa's silhouette against the darkening sky.

A gasp from Caroline Keyes.

"You bitch!" John Swan blurted.

Steele's index finger squeezed the trigger.

Mrs. Porter screamed.

"He hit the fat nooky," Pat Grant muttered, surprised.

Steele grunted as the skyline of the mesa returned to normal. He was unable to tell if he had hit the target or not.

Three more rifle shots sounded in perfect unison, like an echo of his own and the report from the top of the mesa.

The bullets pocked the center of the street, ten feet apart and more than a hundred from where Mrs. Porter was squatting beside the crumpled form of Joanne Brady.

"You stinkin' cow of a friggin' . . ."

Grant was already turning from the window and drawing his revolver. Steele began to whirl part of a second later. His eyes raked from the mesa to the street and received a fleeting but vivid image of Jo-anne Brady, lying face down, with a large stain of darkness in the center of her back—and of Mrs. Porter rising and starting to walk resolutely eastwards again.

Next he saw the enraged Grant, every fiber of his body taut with hatred as the Colt cleared his holster.

Finally, John Swan and Caroline Keyes. The man folded almost double on the bed, his uninjured hand a fraction of an inch away from where his revolver lay on a filthy blanket. The woman stooped over him, both her hands still wrapped around the handle of the knife she had thudded into his back.

Steele's right hand sped away from the barrel of the rifle and chopped downwards, the fingers and thumb pushed out straight from the palm.

"I only . . ." Swan began, snapping up his head to show his agony and sorrow-contorted features to the men at the window.

"He was gonna . . ." Caroline Keyes released her double handed grip on the knife and threw herself backwards.

Grant's gun cracked at the same instant that Swan died.

The thin man's eyes clouded and stared and his head fell forward. His reaching hand was involuntarily withdrawn.

Grant's bullet buried itself into the floorboards four feet away from where the girl fell, unbalanced by the speed of her backward leap.

Steele's damaging hand formed into a claw which closed over the smoking gun and wrenched it from Grant's grasp.

For long moments the freckle-faced man felt no pain at the point where the chopping blow had smashed into his wrist. For his anger was too powerful to allow his mind the experience of any other emotion. For perhaps a full two seconds he glared at the cowering girl. He might have lunged at her had he not felt drawn to look at the Virginian and seen that Steele was unmoved by his murderous fury. Then he heard the soft-spoken revelation.

"Reckon there's just the one man up there, feller."

Grant continued to stare at the Virginian. And Steele saw from the other man's eyes the turmoil that was erupting in his mind as he struggled to assimilate the implications of the comment against the broiling rage demanding an outlet.

"The bitch backstabbed John," Grant gasped at length.

"He was goin' for his gun," the girl choked out. "I thought he was gonna blast you while you was . . ."

"One feller with six rifles," Steele went on in the same even tone. "One in his hands. The other five fixed in the rocks. I reckon he's working the triggers with cords."

Caroline Keyes was still concerned about Grant, even though he was half turned towards Steele and she could see only his profile. Hard anger and deep hatred continued to be inscribed on his face. She remained curled on the floor in the fetal position, her arms around her legs, fingers interlocked.

Grant's eyes showed understanding and surprise as he listened to Steele. But his mind stayed with the killing of John Swan.

"Why'd she do that, Steele?" he asked, his voice strangely querulous, almost child-like. "Why should she give a frig about us?"

" 'Cause of what he done to me!" Caroline excused plaintively, and started to move. She uncurled her body and stood up. Her fingers worked on the buttons of the jacket Steele had given her. And when she was erect, she took hold of each side and jerked them apart, exposing the circles of crusted blood which marked the cuts on her breasts. Her voice got stronger. "And he was just gettin' started! If there was just me and him left here in this stinkin' town, just think what he'd have done to me!"

Grant shook his head as the final ray of the day's sun was cut off by the western horizon. The gesture coincided with a clearing of his mind. And one vivid thought struck him.

"What if it was Swan who took the money?"

"I'm still alive up here!"

Both Steele and the girl had opened their mouths to respond to Grant's question. But their captor at the top of the mesa spoke first, his booming voice as strong as it had ever been. But there was a different quality to it. The Virginian forgot what he had been about to say to Grant as he listened intently to the booming voice: trying to decide whether it was physical pain or mental torment which gave it a different tone.

"The woman! I ain't gonna shoot you. You're gonna die anyway. Out there you'll die and the buzzards and coyotes'll eat the meat off your bones. So are them that're left. Don't you count on no help comin'. You'll die as sure as the woman if you don't give me what I want!"

Silence again. Which seemed more intent than it had ever been as the gathering darkness of twilight was gradually brightened by the glow of the full moon.

With the night came cold. And Caroline Keyes hurriedly refastened the jacket buttons and turned up the lapels.

Steele looked from Grant to the girl and back again. He shivered, the same as they did, as the air temperature abruptly dropped and he felt the sweat dry on his skin. But fear was equally responsible for the tremors moving their flesh—all of it triggered by the disembodied voice which seemed to be making its predictions from heaven itself.

And the Virginian pressed the Colt revolver back into Grant's unexpectant hand before turning to lean out of the window. A faint evening breeze stirred the dust on the street and blew it over the slumped inertness of Joanne Brady. Some particles continued to float freely. Many adhered to the fresh blood staining the girl's jacket. Far beyond where she lay, Mrs. Porter continued on her unmolested journey, striding out purposefully towards a destination she would never reach on foot. She looked very frail in the blue moonlight.

"How long you known that, Steele?" Grant asked, and there was weariness in his voice.

"It matter, feller?"

"To Billy and John. The fat nooky out there on the street. Maybe they'd still have been alive if we'd known we was just up against Hayes and a bundle of smart tricks."

"You care, feller?" He withdrew his head and closed the window on the night. "Or you?" he added to Caroline Keyes.

"I just want outta this town," the girl replied dully.

"I want that," Grant said. Then his tone sharpened as Caroline started towards the bed where Swan was still folded in the frozen attitude of death. "No, sweetheart! You ain't gettin' no more chances to back-stab nobody."

It was enough for him merely to drape a hand over his holstered gun. For the girl came to a weary halt. "What would you have done?" she asked dully. "After what that bastard done to me? And the rest waitin' in line for a turn. I seen the knife on the floor and I took it."

"I don't give a shit about that!" Grant responded. "Just know you killed John Swan and that I didn't back-track Hayes Elliott. Which I figure means you just cut me outta the money, sweetheart."

"You killed his brother!" Caroline accused. "How d'you know it wasn't Billy took the money?"

"Accident. Wasn't meant to happen. But what you done to John—that weren't no accident."

Both were talking in soft tones. But, as the exchange progressed, menace began to coat Grant's words. The girl heard this and watched his draped gun hand with mounting anxiety. She glimpsed the impassive face and frame of Steele out of the corner of her eye and fastened on a chance to divert Grant's threatening attention away from herself.

"What about him?" she muttered with a toss of her head which set her long hair swaying across her back. "He ain't all he seems, I bet. Way he's been actin'. Why'd he keep you from shootin' me? You oughta be worryin' about him instead of me, I figure."

Grant's feelings towards the girl had been inspired by a bleak desire for revenge. Now, as he turned his head and received the same impression of Steele as she got, he realized the futility of what had been concerning him. Caroline recognized the change which had come over the freckle-faced man and pressed on to build up the point she thought she had won.

"People been dyin' all around him and he ain't done nothin' to try and stop it! And he's smart, there ain't no denyin' that! And mean, and a killer. Yet he ain't done no killin' himself. Nor tried to get away from Rain. How d'we know he ain't got the money? How d'we

126

know he wasn't really headin' here in the first place? Why, he might've found out about the meetin' Hayes set up. Come here to kill everyone so he wouldn't have to always be lookin' over his shoulder. Only we done all the killin' for him."

She had started out speaking with forceful conviction. But while Steele remained icily calm and Grant's face showed greater and greater doubt, she came to realize the fatuousness of what she was saying. But, at least, she had succeeded in neutralizing the tension which had seemed to have a palpable presence in the rapidly cooling room.

"You all through?" Steele asked into the silence.

She nodded, suddenly docile. "Dammit, how can anyone think straight after all that's happened?"

"The dude can, I figure," Grant said, faintly resentful. "Which is why he's still alive. You and me, sweetheart . . . we just got dumb luck."

Caroline nodded again and joined Grant in eyeing the Virginian expectantly as the freckle-faced man recalled, "You said you had a plan for when night came, Steele?"

Steele pursed his lips and moved to the bed. The corpse of John Swan remained doubled over and his dead flesh had not yet begun to stiffen. He used the rifle as a lever in a double-handed grip, to tip the body on to its side. Gravity took over then, to send Swan off the edge of the bed and into an untidy heap on the floor. Two pairs of surprised eyes continued to watch Steele as he claimed the bed, resting his back against the headboard and holding the Colt Hartford across his stomach.

"Little water in one of the canteens," he announced. "I'm not greedy. Just take the bed."

"That's your friggin' plan?" Grant snarled, finding it difficult to find the energy to raise fresh anger. "To rest up and hope that bastard comes down after us?"

"I'm not counting on that, feller," Steele answered.

"So what the hell are you countin' on, mister?" Caroline Keyes blurted.

The Virginian yawned and moved the back of his hat against the headboard to tilt the front brim down over his forehead. "Right now," he answered wearily, "Sheep."

# CHAPTER TWELVE

In war, if a man was to survive, he had to learn many lessons in addition to those designed to teach him how to kill the enemy. He had also to be schooled—or to school himself—in the arts of defense. And in this field a highly developed sixth sense to the threat of danger was preeminent. Adam Steele commanded such a sense.

While he was awake, it was difficult to discern—for he concealed his constant state of alertness behind a shield of easy-going nonchalance. But, when he slept, the signs showed. His breathing rate revealed it was a shallow sleep which rested him. And the tight grip he maintained on the Colt Hartford and the way his skin stretched taut over the bone structure of his face gave strong hints that he was poised for instant reaction to anything that should disturb him.

These signs did not lie. The Virginian never slept deeply, whatever the circumstances. And when he awoke, whether voluntarily or because he sensed danger, it was always to instant and total recall, with his reflexes primed to react in a split second to any potential danger.

As he drifted into sleep on the bed in the padre's house of Rain, he was aware of the disgruntled voices of Grant and Caroline. He listened only to their tone and not to the words spoken. Then there were movements within the room. Footfalls and the dry cracks of small bones in legs. The slop of meager water in a canteen. The short-lived gurgles of the liquid flowing down parched throats. Weary sighs as his fellow occupants of the room settled themselves—the man by the window and the girl close to the door—for as much of the night as Steele would allow to slip by before he was ready to move.

Some more talk. And again the Virginian ignored the subject matter of the conversation and allowed only the tones of their voices into his mind. Resentful. Then a short period of anger. Weariness. A rebuke from the man to the girl. Silence.

He awoke and shivered, but the cold of night took the edge off his thirst. And the stink of the decomposing bodies of the Swan brothers was a barrier to hunger pangs. The moon was glitteringly bright and enough of its light filtered in through the dusty window for Steele to be able to pick out the features of the room.

Caroline Keyes was curled up in a ball beside the door, breathing deeply and regularly in sleep. Pat Grant sat on the floor with his back against the bureau, from where he could watch the girl, Steele and a section of the mesa top. A Winchester rifle was resting across his thighs, held loosely in place by one hand.

He was not asleep.

"You knew I'd keep my eye on the back-stabbin' bitch, didn't you?" he accused as Steele sat up and swung his legs over the side of the bed, being careful not to step on the rigor-stiffened corpse of John Swan.

He was right, and this fact had contributed to the Virginian's peace of mind while he slept. Ever since Al Root died, the Swans had looked upon Grant as their leader. But the freckle-faced man had lacked confidence in his own abilities, constantly seeking the advice of Steele by glance or word.

"On account of I'm with you, but she's with nobody," Grant went on in the same resentful tone as Steele rose from the bed and crossed to the bureau without replying.

Grant got painfully and wearily to his feet and moved to the window. He rubbed the area around his leg wound as he surveyed the entire length of the mesa top.

"I reckon, feller," Steele allowed and, resting his rifle, he took off his hat—but not his gloves—and stooped over the basin. The scummy water was cold and served its intended purpose of ridding Steele of the final remnants of sleep as he splashed it over his bristled face.

"She's gotta be crazy, you know that? Comin' all the way down here from Kansas in that crazy dancehall girl's dress. With hardly no supplies . . ."

"On account I didn't have hardly no money left, mister!" Caroline Keyes defended bitterly as she extricated herself from her sleeping posture. "After that bastard Hayes Elliott took all I had to stake him. What I had I spent on a horse and supplies for the trip down here. I didn't figure it'd take this long to get rich. And the dress was the only one I had left after I sold all the . . ."

"Hey, where you goin'?" Grant cut in sharply.

Steele had wiped his face with a shirt sleeve, put on his hat, picked up his rifle and started for the door.

"Out of this town, feller," he replied from the doorway. "I'll take the east end of the mesa. You take the west."

"What about me?" the girl demanded.

"Easy as that?" Grant rasped with a scornful scowl.

"Hayes'll just let us get away with it this time? Won't start blastin' like he did before?"

Steele sighed. "I slept. She slept. You stayed awake. You're tired. We're not. Just the one man up on the mesa. Maybe he's sleeping. Maybe he hasn't been sleeping at all. Or maybe he's had some rest and is awake now."

Grant and Caroline Keyes were both showing him puzzled looks.

"He's either real tired, fast asleep or well rested," the Virginian amplified.

"You been sayin' a lot of maybes, Steele," Grant growled.

The Virginian shrugged. "I reckon they're better than the certainty we had a few hours ago—that he was wide awake and watching."

Grant thought about this for a few moments, then nodded. But he was still anxious.

"What about me?" the girl said again, more insistently. "I can shoot. You've seen that."

"Yeah, Steele," Grant said. "We can't leave her here with all these damn guns."

Caroline scowled, resentful of the connotation the freckled-faced man had placed upon her claim.

"Never planned on you staying down here," Steele told her. "Up to you. Which one of us you want to take you for a moonlight walk?"

"I ain't takin' her!" Grant barked. "I don't wanna have to keep my eyes on her while Hayes is gunnin' for me."

Steele stepped back from the doorway and waited for the girl to step across the threshold in front of him. "Looks like I'm your escort, ma'am," he said with a bleak smile.

"And I'm your prisoner—unless you let me have a gun," she muttered miserably.

"I can see I haven't captured your heart," Steele responded, strengthening his tacit command by waving the rifle towards the doorway. "I wouldn't like for you to put a bullet in mine."

"Why should I . . ." she started, her voice rising.

"I can think of a hundred thousand reasons!" Steele cut in on her, his tone a soft rasp. Then he moderated his voice as he shared a warning look between the man and the girl. "And let's keep the noise down from here on in. The moon's near as bright as the sun was last time. But the shadows are deeper." He was looking directly at the nervous Grant now. "Use them where you can. Keep to the rear of the buildings on this side of the street until the edge of town. Then cross fast. But quiet. If he's awake up there, he'll be watching this house. If you get to the far side of the street, head for the base of the bluff. Then along it and round the side until you find a way up."

"If he spots us and starts blastin'?" Grant asked tensely.

"Hope he misses you, feller. And keep going and hoping."

Grant glanced at the corpses of Billy and John Swan, scowling at the sight and smell of them. He swallowed hard. "And at the top?"

"You and him, me and him or both of us and him, feller," Steele replied evenly.

Grant licked his dry lips. "I think we oughta stick together, Steele."

"You're too tired to think, feller. It could get you killed. Same as the man on the top of the mesa. Let's go."

He gestured with the rifle again and Caroline Keyes

133

went out on to the landing. Steele followed her and Grant brought up the rear. At the foot of the stairway, the Virginian took the lead, going through a doorway and across the kitchen to the rear exit of the house.

The back lots of the buildings in Rain had once been as neatly laid out as the front gardens, with picket fences dividing the properties. Progress was slow as Grant headed away from the padre's house in one direction and Steele and the girl moved in the opposite. They had to swing up and over the fences which still stood and to step across those which had fallen. All the timber was rotted and dried by exposure to weather and a single misplaced step would snap brittle wood with the sound of a rifle shot in the total silence of the cold Texas night.

Steele ignored Grant and concentrated all his attention on the circumstances which were within his control—the steady and silent progress of himself and the girl. Even when they reached the final house on the north side of the street—still pungent with the sickly sweet smell of the long dead horse—he did not look back over his shoulder to check on the whereabouts of Grant.

For a few moments, he paused at the front corner of the house to peer up at the top of the mesa opposite the center of town. Stars glinted against blackness. The rock of the mesa had a faint silver sheen in the blue moonlight. Nothing moved.

Except the flesh of Steele and the girl and Pat Grant. Each tremor was caused by either cold or fear or a combination of the two. Only for a moment did the Virginian allow himself to indulge in futile memories of the well-worn sheepskin coat that was lost forever. It was equally unproductive to experience regret for having loaned his suit jacket to the girl behind him.

"Zig-zag if he starts shooting," he murmured. "Come on."

He lunged out into the open—first beside the garden fencing, then across the street, finally another stretch of fence before he reached the cover of the house on the south side. His footfalls sounded deafeningly loud in his own ears. From the corner of his eye he saw that Grant had been awaiting his move and was sprinting over the street at the far end of town. He could not hear the girl running bare-footed behind him but felt her slam into him as he came to an abrupt halt in cover. She bounced off him and hit the side of the house. Her mouth was gaped wide to vent a sound of pain as he spun towards her. His cold eyes locked on her gaze and silenced her.

"He's asleep," she rasped after her lips had come together, the scream muted to nothing more than a soft sigh of relief.

"Or waiting until we get close," Steele growled.

During the many centuries of the mesa's existence on the Texas plain, the wild weather of pre-history had altered its shape. Many rocks had been split or crumbled from its face and these were now scattered across the dust-layered area between its base and the abandoned town. The distance to be crossed was about two hundred feet and Steele reached the foot of the bluff in short spurts of speed interrupted by pauses at the largest boulders. The girl stayed far enough behind him to avoid collisions. To the west, Grant imitated the Virginian's actions.

No rifle shot exploded.

The sweat of tension and fear dried instantly on trembling flesh.

A lone man and a man and a girl picked their way carefully and silently along the base of the bluff. Almost a half mile to the east and to the west. Then south.

Grant's journey was the shorter for he found a way up just a few yards along the western face of the mesa. Steele and Caroline Keyes had to move all the way around the curving eastern end and then go west along the southern side before they could start to climb. Over another half mile in all.

But their route to the top was easier. A wide natural trail of pitted rock. Steep, but not too steep for a wagon and team to negotiate as they could see from the wheel and hoofmarks in dust-filled indentations in the rock.

At the top, Steele halted again, to peer cautiously across the weather-ravaged surface of the mesa towards the campsite on the far side.

There was a buckboard over there, with a single horse hitched to a rear wheel. Beside the wagon was a strange looking contraption—a large cone perhaps six feet long and with a mouth some six feet in diameter. It stood on a three-legged support, its mouth directed up at the sky. Behind this was a pup tent.

The camp was some ten yards back from the top of the bluff—far enough away so that it could not be seen from the town below. Much closer to the edge were the five rifles, their barrels wedged between natural formed rocks or supported by man-fashioned arrangements. Moveable timber frames clamped the stocks in place so that the angle and range of fire could be adjusted.

Steele had been wrong in one of his guesses. Fine wire rather than cord had been used to trigger the Winchesters. He saw it gleaming in the moonlight which illuminated the entire surface of the mesa top as he and the girl moved closer to the campsite: the wires stretching from the rifles, around small stakes driven into the rock, to an elongated hump at the edge of the mesa which had provided cover for the man who devised the scheme.

"He always was the smartest sonofabitch I ever knew," Caroline rasped.

"You ever known him to sleep this soundly?" Steele murmured.

She swallowed hard and compressed her lips.

They had covered half the distance to the pup tent, buckboard, horse and odd-looking cone. Over to the left, Pat Grant was matching their pace, taking care not to reach the campsite before they did. Both men had their rifles leveled and cocked, fingers curled to the triggers.

The two men and the girl sweated and shivered. The girl breathed heavily. The men could not avoid the sounds of their boots on the rocky surface.

"Come outta there with your friggin' hands up, Hayes!" Grant snarled.

He had reached the side of the buckboard and crouched beside it.

Caroline Keyes caught her breath and Steele scowled. Both of them were in the open.

The horse, which had watched the flanking advances in silence, snorted.

A rifle cracked.

"Shit!" Grant said shrilly as he was forced into a sitting position by the bullet which tunneled into his belly.

His rifle clanged against a wheelrim and bounced to the ground.

The horse remained calm at the sound of the shot. And began to munch from a bale of hay on the bed of the buckboard.

Steele whirled into a half turn and then forward again—pushing the stock of the Colt Hartford out to the side. The rosewood with the inscribed gold plate screwed to it thudded into the small of Caroline's back. She screamed her pain and alarm—and was forced by

137

the impact of the blow to lunge forward. Her scream rose in shrillness as she crashed into the pup tent and fell across it.

The support pole tilted and stakes were wrenched from the ground. The canvas shelter collapsed.

The man who had fired blindly from inside at the sound of Grant's voice vented a howl of mixed emotions. Pain and surprise and disappointment and rage.

Steele saw a booted foot revealed by the collapsing canvas and lunged forward. One gloved hand left the rifle as he stooped and gripped the ankle. He halted and then powered into a reverse move: to jerk the man out from under the canvas and the struggling girl.

An old man. More than sixty, with just the one leg Steele had taken hold of. The other had been amputated above the knee. With a bald head and a wizened face—terribly scarred by a thousand old wounds where he had been peppered by buckshot. Much fresher was the wound on the right side of his chest, marked by the ragged hole in his shirt front with a wide area of crusted blood around it.

"You ain't Hayes!" Grant gasped incredulously as he stared wide-eyed under the buckboard.

The old man's hands were empty now, his rifle somewhere under the fallen tent on which Caroline Keyes lay, frozen into immobility by the same degree of shock which gripped Grant.

Steele released his grip on the ankle and came erect, pursing his lips as he canted the Colt Hartford to his left shoulder.

The old man sat up, in great pain from the recent wound delivered by Steele's final shot from Rain. But he was able to form his ghastly scarred features into a grin of triumph as he swung his head to look at the

138

freckle-faced man with fresh blood spreading wide on the front of his shirt.

Grant's shock expanded. "We thought you was dead!" he croaked. Some blood bubbled up from his throat with the words and spilled out over his lower lip.

"Soon will be, I guess." His voice sounded nothing like it had to the ears of those he had trapped in Rain. And not just because of his pain and weakness. "Almost was after you and them other fellers robbed that express car up in Missouri. Been better for me if all them bullets and all that buckshot had killed me, I guess. Better for you and your buddies, that's for sure."

He laughed. Just a short sound before his agony curtailed it.

"Revenge is all?" Steele asked levelly.

"Money don't buy a man a new leg or a new face, mister," the old man answered, looking up at the Virginian. "Not even all that money they stole."

"But how?" Grant croaked.

The girl continued in her frozen attitude. Her green eyes had the familiar stare in them, but she was gazing at something a lot closer than infinity now.

"Got to Elliott first," the old man answered. And there was pride in his voice and his expression as he kept his attention on Steele. "Gave him some real hell before he told me about what he planned to do here at Rain. Killed him then. Cut off his hands and buried him. Someplace between Abilene and Wichita. Come across Flint and Sullivan a lot closer to here. Cut off their hands before I killed 'em. Fittin' punishment for thieves, I figured."

"You've done a lot of figuring, feller," Steele said, glancing about the campsite and the aimed guns beyond.

"Yeah. But then I ain't really a killer, mister. Shoot a rifle real good, but only used it for huntin' before this. Set all this up to make the bastards suffer. Safer for me, too, I guess. What with me havin' just the one good leg." The short laugh again, cut off by pain. "Just the one leg."

"The money!" Grant demanded. "What about the friggin' money?"

"Elliott told me one of you boys took it," the old man replied with disinterest. "He sure didn't have it. If he did have, he'd sure have give it to me. What I was doin' to him. It was what he told me about his plan that give me the idea for all this."

"It weren't me!" Grant pleaded, switching his pain-wracked gaze to Steele.

"Just sorry about the stage driver and that woman I shot," the old man said regretfully. "But I didn't want no law comin' here until the whole bunch that hit the express car was dead. But a man can't plan for everythin', can he?"

"No, feller," Steele answered.

"Sure can't plan the time he's gonna die!" Grant croaked.

His blood-stained right hand had drawn the Colt from his holster. But it was not his gun which exploded. Instead, the old man's Winchester in the rock-steady grip of Caroline Keyes.

Steele had been aware of her slight movements after she emerged from the state of shock. She had managed to keep her punished body motionless while her hands delved under the canvas to locate the rifle. The old man had had time to pump the action before the tent collapsed on him. So all the girl had to do was point the Winchester and squeeze the trigger.

The bullet took Grant in the center of his freckled forehead and he was flung on-to his back.

The horse continued to munch on the hay bale in the rear of the buckboard.

Steele had to shoot her then. Or die himself. For even before Grant's corpse was sprawled full-length beside the quiet horse, the girl was pumping the rifle's lever action and swinging the muzzle towards him.

The Colt Hartford whipped down into the cupped palm. The hammer was already cocked from the advance on the campsite.

He fired from the hip, having to aim wide of the old man, who was as calm as his horse. The bullet drilled into and through her left shoulder. The impact of the lead against her flesh turned her and threw her down. She dropped the Winchester as she screamed, then reached out clawed hands to reclaim it.

Steele elevated the rifle stock to his shoulder and took aim. Three reports sent three bullets smashing into the frame of the Winchester. The distorted lead ricocheted off into the night. The girl threw herself into a roll, a trail of blood marking her retreat from danger.

"It was the old-timer he reckoned to kill, ma'am," the Virginian drawled as he canted the Colt Hartford to his shoulder.

"All right, you bastard! It was me!"

Her roll had ended with her on her back, her pain-contorted face immediately beneath the big one on its stand. So that her screamed admission was bull-horned into a booming distortion of her voice. To reveal why nobody who had known him had been able to realize it had not been Hayes Elliott who taunted them from the top of the mesa.

The strangeness of her own voice frightened Caroline

Keyes for a moment. Until she had jerked out from under the cone and struggled to her feet. Then, as she clutched at her bleeding shoulder and wrenched her gaze away from the cone to Steele, her fear evaporated in the icy cold of night. For she knew her situation was hopeless. She sensed from the nonchalant impassiveness of the Virginian that he was not a man who accepted compromise.

Or perhaps she was as insane as Grant had suggested. Driven into madness by the loneliness and then the horrors of her stay in the abandoned town below the mesa.

"It was true about Hayes and his new woman," she said, slowly and distinctly. "I did make a mistake in blastin' Root. But it didn't matter, 'cause I wanted them all dead. Hayes told his new woman where the money was hid. And I took it and hid it in another place before I come down here."

She was backing away from where the old man sat on the collapsed tent. Steele stood behind it.

"Somewhere no one'll ever find it. You sure won't. No one will!" Her words were coming faster as her tone reached a high shrillness. "I was gonna kill 'em all. Every last one of 'em. Then I was gonna live high. In New York. Or maybe out in Frisco. With no one left alive to start wonderin' how I got the money."

She continued to walk backwards.

"So kill me, mister! You might as well. I'm the reason for all what's happened. And you won't get me alive so as I can talk and tell you where I hid the money?"

"Hold it right there, Caroline," Steele ordered softly. "Take another step and you're dead."

"And the money's gone forever, you stupid sonofa—"

She started another scream then. As her final challenge of a backward step took her over the edge of the mesa. At one moment she was in sight, silhouetted against the star-glinting sky. Then she was gone, the stridency of her scream diminishing as her fall lengthened. There was just a faint thud audible at the top of the mesa as her body was crushed by the impact of hitting the ground at its base.

"That was some lousy warnin' you give her, mister," the wreck of an old man said, as indifferent to her death as he had been at Grant's.

"Reckon it was," the Virginian drawled, pushing the Colt Hartford towards the sky and turning the cylinder to empty out the expended shell cases. "Should make you happy, though. She staked them while they planned the robbery. That's the last one of them dead, feller."

He reloaded, emptying his pants pocket to slot a bullet into each vacant chamber.

The old man shook his head sorrowfully. "Even before I was shot, mister, I'd had my fill of revenge. It was pluggin' that woman in the back that did it, I guess. But for a long time before that the stink from the body of the stage driver was stronger in my nostrils than from any other dead down there."

With the rifle fully loaded, Steele had turned his attention to the horse and buckboard, unhitching the black gelding and fixing him in the traces.

"Know the feeling, feller," he said, and the comment was cryptic to the ears of the old man.

He didn't spend long thinking about it, though. Perhaps because he realized he did not have much time left for anything. Fresh droplets of blood gleamed on the congealed blackness of his jaw.

"You're the kinda man don't show *his* feelin's, mister. Way that girl was talkin', I figured you had an interest in the money she hid."

"Never take anything that isn't mine, feller. Reckoned there would be a reward offered by the express company."

"Sure was. Ten per cent. Put up by the office in Kansas City."

Steele climbed up on to the seat of the buckboard. He had seen several canteens in the back and he raised one of them to his parched lips. The cold water tasted good going down his throat and into his stomach. But it didn't trigger any hunger pangs. Yet, there was a case in the back of the buckboard.

"Lot of money," the Virginian allowed. "But Kansas City is a long way to go. I'm heading east for a while, feller. You want a ride?"

"A couple of miles is all I'd make, mister. Be obliged if you'd leave me to die here."

The talk had spilled more droplets of blood to gleam in the moonlight.

"See you in hell, then."

"A place that'll be filled up with unfriendly faces, that's for sure."

Steele drove down off the mesa without looking back over his shoulder. There were a lot of guns close to where the old man sat on the collapsed tent. But even if he had the strength, he had neither the reason nor the inclination to crawl to one and use it.

As he held the gelding to a straining walk on the steep slope of the natural trail, Steele saw the stalled stage. It was far out to the northwest where the driver had made the mistake of telling his story to the wrong man. The other three horses which had formed the team had been turned loose so there was no need for him to go out to where the stage stood, tiny in perspective, except for his saddle and bedroll. But the horse and buckboard were worth more.

So he turned the gelding towards the east, back-tracking on the trail towards the Fort Worth fork. When the mesa ceased to intervene, he was conscious of the town of Rain at his back. But he never turned to look at it. Soon, the stink of its dead could no longer be detected in the bitterly cold night air.

He did not ask for speed from the gelding and the gray light of dawn was streaking the eastern sky when he reined in the horse beside the old lady. Mrs. Porter had seen him before he picked her out from among the sparse scattering of rocks and desert vegetation.

"This night air has played hell with my stiff joints, young man," she said weakly.

"There'll be a doctor in Fort Worth," he answered.

She seemed twice as thin as he remembered her. And a great deal older. She was coated from head to toe with a layer of gray dust, but the floral hat was still perched squarely on her white hair.

She pulled away from him as he tried to help her climb on to the seat. So he left her alone to do it herself. She grimaced a great deal, then settled on to the seat with a sigh of relief.

"Everyone else is dead," she said, making it a statement rather than a question as he clucked the horse into movement.

"Including the man on the mesa." He squinted at the first rays of the rising sun. "By this time."

She did not reply. Just leaned gratefully against the backrest and held her head high to expose her cold-pinched face to the first warmth of the morning sun.

"That was a real dangerous thing you did, ma'am," Steele told her. "Using the water that way and pretending it was an innocent mistake."

"It made you all start thinkin' of a way out a lot

quicker than you might have otherwise, young man," she replied.

He nudged her shoulder with a canteen. And she opened her eyes for just long enough to see what was offered. Then she snapped them closed again and shook her head.

"Thank you, but no. I just want to reach Fort Worth and get down from this wagon. Then I will not be required to touch or see anythin' that came from that terrible place. Although I fear it will all live in my mind until my dyin' day."

"You'll get over it, ma'am," the Virginian told her evenly as he began to feel his skin and muscles shed their frozen quality in the early sunlight. He flicked the reins to order a trot from the gelding before the heat built up. "In time you'll just recall it as an unpleasant . . ."

**PREVIEW**

The savage saga of a heroic Indian warrior—
and his relentless battle against the
ruthless white man.

by William M. James
Apache

*In the following pages, excerpted from the gripping Apache\* series, you will meet Cuchillo Oro—a fictional character of heroic dimension and power. Cuchillo's strength as an Indian warrior, inspired by such notorious Indian leaders as Cochise and Geronimo, and his knowledge of the white man's ways aids him in his search for a just revenge upon the "White Eyes" for the crimes committed against his people. And though Cuchillo faces death at every turn, the Apache credo of living with honor and dignity gives him the inner strength to carry out his destiny. Here, then, is the often shocking and cruel realism of the Indian wars—and some of the most exciting reading ever to come out of the West!*

In the past, before an Indian-hating horsesoldier had lit the fires of mindless rage in the heart of Cuchillo, the Apache had been just another brave, living in dejected squalor—but peacefully—on the Borderline Rancheria of the Arizona territory, with his gentle wife and their newborn baby.

The threat of an uprising against the White Eyes was always in the air at Borderline, almost as tangible as the smoke from the cooking fires. But Cuchillo, even though he was descended from the great chief Mangas Coloradas, could never be persuaded by the hotheads to take up arms against the oppressors of the Apaches. He elected, instead, to put into practice only the peaceful tenets of his renowned ancestor. . . .

And he shared in the belief of the only White Eyes he called friend—the schoolteacher John Hedges—that the time would come when men of different races would cover tolerance of each other without resort to war.

Much blood would still be coursing through living veins instead of congealing on the dirt of countless battlefields if the evil Lieutenant Cyrus Pinner had not shattered the dream composed of an Indian's teachings and the belief of a White Eyes.

Cuchillo had been falsely accused of stealing an ornate and valuable dagger belonging to Pinner. A man less bigoted than the horsesoldier officer would have examined the facts more closely before taking action. But Pinner, unable to contain his hatred for all Indians, could not even think of giving the benefit of the doubt to one.

A knife and then a gun hacked and blasted the young brave's right hand into virtual uselessness, leaving him with just the third and fourth finger and the thumb, and these almost paralyzed.

Such a punishment would have been cruel enough to a White Eyes victim. To a full-blooded Apache it was utterly barbaric. For it was written that a brave not bodily whole was barred entry to the Land of the Great Spirits when it came his turn to die.

Cuchillo—given his second name of Oro following the incident involving the golden knife—set little store by such tales. After long periods of study in the schoolroom of John Hedges, he had learned to accept and reject by the art of reason those aspects of both the Indian and the White Eyes cultures that either did or did not appeal to him.

So, perhaps, he had never been just another Apache brave when Borderline had been an oasis of uneasy peace. Whatever he had been served to spur his violent response to the torture he suffered. And, for the purely personal purpose of taking his revenge against Pinner, Cuchillo Oro was the fuse that ignited Borderline into an uprising. A man alone in the midst of a bloody battle, he was also alone in experiencing the acid bitterness of personal defeat. The fort from which Borderline had been ruled was reduced to burning rubble. The Apaches won a small triumph at great cost. Pinner was one of the horsesoldiers who survived, to strut in personal victory before the crumpled and blood-run bodies of Cuchillo's wife and baby son.

In grief-striken defeat, Cuchillo had claimed one of the spoils of victory—the golden knife for which he was named and which was the cause of his suffering—claimed by the act of drawing its blade from the still-warm flesh of his dead baby son.

But he could not use it against Pinner, nor could he use any other weapon. His right hand was mutilated and his left had never been trained to work alone. So he had retreated into the mountains of Mexico, there to spend countless hours, days and weeks in schooling himself to become as skilled with his left hand as he had always been with his right. Only when he was completely satisfied that he could gain nothing more from his period of isolation did he return north across the border, to find and to kill Pinner.

He had found him, time and time again. And Pinner had found Cuchillo just as often. Both men were engaged on a bitter vengeance hunt, each for the other. One sought to kill in order to settle an old score, the other because he did not consider the lives of an Apache squaw and child payment enough for a golden knife.

Now, many moons later, it was winter, and even when the sun shone, the air was viciously cold. When the sky was leaden with clouds, when it rained, when there was sleet and this turned to snow, a man alone in the mountains was doomed to die. . . . Unless that man was Cuchillo Oro, the Apache brave wise in the ways of the White Eyes, a brave in his early twenties and extraordinarily tall for one of his race. He stood six-feet-two and was impressively built, with a massive chest and muscular limbs. Deprivation and his chosen life-style had never allowed an ounce of excess fat to form on his body. He was handsome as only an Indian can be, his features fashioned into proud lines. He had narrow, coal-black eyes, a nose with flared nostrils, high cheekbones, a wide mouth and a resolute jaw. Thick hair, as black as his eyes, flowed down to brush at his broad shoulders. His complexion was an even bronze, the taut skin of his face scoured with aging lines before its time. Grief and bitterness, suffering and hatred, had etched his flesh in this way. The white-hot rage generated by mental images of his pain and humiliation at the han[d] of the cruel horsesoldier Pinner renewed his will to su[r]vive—even under the most arduous of circumstance[s] No man could do more than kill him, and he was not afraid to die. He was just desperate to live—to complete the mission of vengeance at which he had failed so often: to kill the hated Cyrus Pinner of the White Eyes cavalry.

But always, Pinner and "Pinner's Indian" eluded the fatal bullet or knife thrust. They searched, came together, clashed and then were driven by circumstances onto different paths again and again, until . . . it finally happened . . . the death the Apache had waited for since he was a warrior of eighteen. With the first plunge of the mighty golden knife into Cyrus Pinner's evil flesh, Cuchillo Oro released his pent-up hatred for the horsesoldier, sending the fatally wounded cavalry officer over the cliffs and into the cold waters of the river.

It was over—the blood feud between himself and Pinner—he should be filled with a great satisfaction. He had prayed for it, longed to make the last atonement for his wife and child. . . . Yet, oddly, he felt empty, drained. The expected elation was not there. Cuchillo was suddenly angry. Somehow, he felt cheated. Was this all there was?

Avenging his avowed enemy is not enough for the embittered brave. As long as there are White Eyes left to ravage the land of his ancestors, the warrior must continue his battle. With his proud blood rising, Cuchillo Oro, the grandson of the wise chieftain Mangas Coloradas, renews his promise for revenge. This time there is no turning back—not for the Apache, and not for those who have persecuted his people!

# George G. Gilman

# STEELE

## More bestselling western adventure from Pinnacle, America's #1 series publisher!